THE
MERMAN
and
THE BOOK OF POWER

Also by Musharraf Ali Farooqi

Novels

Between Clay and Dust
The Story of a Widow
Salar Jang's Passion

For Children

Tik-Tik, the Master of Time
Rabbit Rap: A Fable for the 21st Century
The Cobbler's Holiday or Why Ants Don't Wear Shoes
The Amazing Moustaches of Moochander the Iron Man and Other Stories

Translations

Hoshruba—The Land & the Tilism by Muhammad Husain Jah
The Adventures of Amir Hamza by Ghalib Lakhnavi and Abdullah Bilgrami
Rococo and Other Worlds: Selected Poetry of Afzal Ahmed Syed
The Beast by Syed Muhammad Ashraf

The MERMAN and the BOOK OF POWER

a qissa

~

TOLD *by*

MUSHARRAF ALI FAROOQI

ALEPH BOOK COMPANY
An independent publishing firm
promoted by *Rupa Publications India*

First published in India in 2019
by Aleph Book Company
7/16 Ansari Road, Daryaganj
New Delhi 110 002

Copyright © Musharraf Ali Farooqi 2019

The author has asserted his moral rights.

This is a work of fiction. Names, characters,
places and incidents are either the product of the
author's imagination or are used fictitiously and any
resemblance to any actual persons, living or dead,
events or locales is entirely coincidental.

All rights reserved.

No part of this publication may be reproduced,
transmitted, or stored in a retrieval system, in any
form or by any means, without permission in
writing from Aleph Book Company.

ISBN: 978-93-88292-93-1

1 3 5 7 9 10 8 6 4 2

Printed at Parksons Graphics Pvt. Ltd, India

For sale in the Indian subcontinent excluding
Pakistan.

This book is sold subject to the condition that it
shall not, by way of trade or otherwise, be lent,
resold, hired out, or otherwise circulated without
the publisher's prior consent in any form of binding
or cover other than that in which it is published.

For Rizwan

Author's Note

This book merges the parallel histories, myths, and multiple personas for Apollonius of Tyana, Hermes Trismegistus, and Alexander the Great in the Western and Eastern literary canon, and the various religious, occult, and apocalyptic traditions associated with them. Among the texts consulted to research these characters, the following were mainly relied upon: *Sikandar Nama* (The Adventures of Alexander) by Nizami Ganjavi (Matba Majeedi, 1931), *Theios Sophistès: Essays on Flavius Philostratus' Vita Apollonii*, edited by Kristoffel Demoen and Danny Praet (Brill, 2009), and *Apollonius of Tyana: The Philosopher-reformer of the First Century A.D.* by George Robert Stowe Mead (London Theosophical Publishing Society, 1901). The events leading up to the fall of Amorium are based on recorded history as related by Tabari in *Tarikh al-Rusul wa al-Muluk* (History of the Prophets and Kings) and by Masudi in *Muruj al-zahab wa maadin al-jawhar* (The Meadows of Gold and Mines of Gems). The details of Abu-Tammam's panegyric are taken from *The Poetics of Islamic Legitimacy: Myth, Gender, and Ceremony in the Classical Arabic Ode* by Suzanne Pinckney Stetkevych (Indiana University Press,

2002). The occult text *Kitab-e Zakhira-e Sikandar Zulqarnain* (The Book of the Treasure of Alexander the Bicornous) was, according to one tradition, discovered from a monastery in Amorium after its fall to the Abbasid armies. The passage titled 'The Compact' gives the translation made from the Persian and Urdu language versions of its epilogue modified in the interests of the story. Some events that happened during Caliph Mamun's reign have been shifted to Caliph Wathiq's reign. The fictionalized accounts of Wathiq's dream and Khwarizmi and Sallam's journeys to discover Alexander's Rampart are based on historic events whose details could be read in *Gog and Magog in Early Eastern Christian and Islamic Sources: Sallam's Quest for Alexander's Wall* by Emeri van Donzel and Andrea Schmidt (Brill, 2010). The information about the marvels, often fictionalized, was mostly drawn from *Ajaib al-makhluqat wa gharaib al-maujudat* (Marvels of Things Created and Miraculous Aspects of Things Existing) by Qazwini, translated into the Urdu by Tasadduq Hussain (Naval Kishore Press, 1913), and *Maaloomat al-Aafaq* (The Information Regarding the Heavens) by Aminuddin Khan, translated into the Urdu by Mehdi Ali Khan (Naval Kishore Press, 1873) as *Matla-ul-Ajaib*. An abridged version of the merman's story was published under the title, 'Qazwini and the Man of the Sea,' in the daily *Dawn* of 16 February 2014, as part of my fortnightly 'Magic Lantern' series of stories.

Musharraf Ali Farooqi

Characters

RULERS

Alexander of Macedon
356–323 BCE
Conqueror. Built Rampart against Gog and Magog.

Caliph Mamun
Reigned: 813–833 CE
Breached Cheops's Pyramid in quest for ancient wisdom.

Caliph Motasem
Reigned: 833–842 CE
Sacked Amorium.

Caliph Wathiq
Reigned: 842–847 CE
Sent missions to the Grotto of Seven Sleepers & Alexander's Rampart.

PHILOSOPHERS & FUNCTIONARIES

Apollonius of Tyana
15–100 CE
Philosopher and Occultist. Miracle-worker.

Khwarizmi
c. 780–c. 850 CE
Polymath. Visited the Grotto of Sleepers of Ephesus.

Sallam Tarjuman
?–c. 850 CE
Linguist. Surveyed Alexander's Rampart.

Khadish
c. 800–844 CE
Abbasid era philosopher. Heretic. Propagated the theory of adversarial creators and protocols of existence.

Caliph Muqtadir
Reigned: 908–932 CE
Sent mission to confirm report of Commander of Gog and Magog.

Caliph Qadir
Reigned: 991–1031 CE
Buried the Abbasid occult manuscripts collection.

Caliph Mustasim
Reigned: 1242–1258 CE
Last Abbasid caliph. Killed by Hulagu Khan.

Hulagu Khan
Reigned: 1256–1265 CE
Conqueror. Founder of Ilkhanid Mongol dynasty.

Juvayni
Reigned: 1259–c. 1283 CE
Governor of Baghdad. Historian of the Mongols.

Ibn Fadlan
877–c. 925 CE
Jurist. Headed mission to confirm report of Commander of Gog and Magog.

Qazwini
1203–1283 CE
Polymath, jurist, and cosmographer.

Tusi
1201–1274 CE
Polymath. Founded observatory in Azerbaijan.

Chapter 1

Long before the morning of Wednesday, 13 February 1258 dawned on Baghdad, rumours had spread that the signs of the promised End Time had been revealed. Two weeks earlier, the Mongol armies had arrived and laid siege to the city. The ferocity of their advance had convinced the citizens of Baghdad that they were the manifestation of the End Time creatures Gog and Magog, imprisoned by the legendary King Alexander behind a Rampart. It was said that their faces, red as the flames of hell, seemed buried between their shoulders. Their lice-covered, steely bodies gave off a dreadful odour, as their fierce, small eyes moved alertly in their sockets. Thick sideburns protruded like snakes from sheepskin caps covering their shaven heads. In the night, their teeth and talons had glowed as they slunk outside the city walls like malevolent wolves.

Bred in darkness, the unbridled horde had reportedly brought down the Rampart with claws that pierced steel. They had arrived, as foretold, on wild horses, which overtook the wind, carrying sharp scimitars penetrating the heaviest mail, and shooting arrows that never missed their mark. Led by the bandy-legged, snub-nosed, and squint-eyed Hulagu Khan, in whom they had found the commander they sought, the foe had ridden unopposed, gathering all the enemies of the True Faith in the sweep of their murderous advance.

They besieged the city by encircling it with a ditch and erecting a palisade. Earlier, they had filled up the irrigation canals, while their hordes destroyed the dams built on the Tigris and Euphrates.

The citizens of the besieged city heard the grinding sounds of rolling siege engines, fortifications being struck with mangonels, and crashing walls burying panicked cries. The assault did not cease from the hours of light to darkness. From one day to another the ballistae pounded the city walls. After a week-long relentless attack and torrential shower of stones, the city's defences fell; it surrendered after five days.

With frightened eyes the citizens watched the caliph's three thousand emissaries—scholars, merchants, and high officials among them—going outside the city to beg reprieve for the citizens. A day earlier Hulagu Khan had spurned the caliph's offer to confer on him the title of Sultan, and have his name proclaimed at Friday sermons from Baghdad mosques.

The enemy commanders conducted the procession of the caliph's emissaries through the palisades, and allowed them to cross the ditch. When they had moved past the long row of standard bearers the trap was sprung. They were encircled by lance-bearers who had stood still, the points of their weapons concealed with banners. Those watching from the city walls shouted in terror as they saw the dark shadow of a column of troopers advancing towards the besieged men. The ground shook from the pounding of hooves as the troopers shot through the lanes made by the pointing lances and beheaded the first few rows of the emissaries. They wheeled their mounts around, crushing the writhing bodies, and galloped away through the path opened for them by the lancers, who again barred it swiftly. In the time it took for the convulsing torsos and burbling heads to become still, the troopers charged again, beheading many hundreds more. As they turned back this time, the sky above them darkened from the barrage of arrows, breaking the spines and shattering the skulls of those left standing. There was no escape. All three thousand men sent by the caliph were mowed down by flashing blades and flying arrows before the eyes of those watching from the city walls.

For two nights afterwards the enemy was silent. It was said they were feasting on the corpses of the slain. On the third night the besieged people again heard their cries. The mangonels fired and made large holes in the city walls for the attackers' ingress. A flaming arrow struck the Abbasids' black square banner with the eagle emblem and set it afire. Woven with gold and silver it took a few moments for the flames to consume the metallic threads, which glowed like fiery letters before becoming molten darkness.

In the city it was widely believed that the Judgment Day was upon them. The faithful readied people for impending death, instructing mothers to give their infants the last suck, and proselytizing the faithful not to resist, but to prostrate themselves before the enemy ushering in the Apocalypse.

As the call to the afternoon prayer was being given, the attack came. Amidst horrific yells, the enemy swarmed through the breached walls and swept into the city. Their waves left behind headless men spouting blood who groped about the streets, before falling down writhing and becoming still. The murderers' faces glowed with bloodlust; they growled, shouted, and grunted malevolently as they dragged women out from their shelters. They snatched children suckling from their mothers' breasts and brought other women into premature labour. The panicked cries and screams of women were drowned out by the enemy's excited cries, the drumbeat of hooves, and the violent neighing of horses. Every avenue of flight was sealed. As the citizens sought escape, circulating between alleys and passageways, they were hunted and massacred like cattle.

Days later, the caliph was dragged out from imprisonment to witness the beheading of his sons. The killing of the caliph induced fear in the enemy because it was said an earthquake would level all humanity or a giant asteroid smite earth if the blood of God's vicegerent were spilled. At Hulagu Khan's orders the caliph was rolled up in a carpet, crushed by bludgeons, and then trodden under horses' hooves until his every bone was shattered with no blood spilled. Baghdad's last Abbasid caliph and his empire were dead.

The Baghdad massacre, in which eight hundred thousand men, women, and children were slain, had continued for five days. In the unbearable stench of putrefaction Hulagu Khan moved his camp upwind from the city.

Another invasion of the city by the vultures, carrion-eaters and vermin was underway.

Chapter 2

A little over a year after the sack of Baghdad by the Mongols, on Thursday, 24 July 1259, a noisy crowd followed a strange creature some Mediterranean fishermen had brought overland to Baghdad in a canopied boat filled with water and fitted with wheels. To the beat of the kettledrums heralding their progress, the procession moved slowly in the blistering heat towards the governor's palace where the creature was to be presented to Governor Juvayni, a man both feared and revered as Hulagu Khan's foremost official.

People climbed over each other's shoulders to catch a glimpse of the creature in the boat and cried out excitedly, as the palace gates opened to admit the fishermen's procession. The drums stopped beating as the gates closed, but the crowd stayed to hear of the creature's fate.

Like others present at court, Governor Juvayni felt an ill omen at the first sight of the creature whose bulging eyes, protruding from a forehead as wide and high as a bull's, crowned a face lined with a network of thick veins. Sharp canines hung over his lower lip. Broad shouldered, with sinewy arms, the merman's powerful, scarred torso was partially covered by long, dark hair trailing to his navel. His unified lower body was covered with scales. A cloud of flies and the ripe smell of fish enveloped him. Submerged in the felt and leather-lined boat, he haughtily leaned back against the bow, without displaying fear or concern about his fate.

The leader of the fishermen who had found him caught in their nets bowed before the governor, and after a litany of praises addressed to Juvayni, introduced the creature as Gujastak, meaning the Accursed, a name given him by the fishermen because the merman's presence frightened away the fish in the sea for miles.

Governor Juvayni waited for his excited courtiers to fall quiet so that he could dismiss with a small reward the fishermen along with the merman. He wished the creature out of his sight. Pressing matters of state needed his attention. Tasked with restoring Baghdad's infrastructure and reviving its economy, his hours were taken up with supervising the city's reconstruction, and rebuilding the commerce and trade routes devastated in the Mongol attack on the city. Agriculture had been badly impaired from the destruction of the dams on the Tigris and Euphrates, and he had the added responsibility of overseeing its revival. The assignment had come in the middle of his work on the universal history which he believed would keep alive his name, and inform the futurity of how the wise military and foreign policies of the Mongols influenced the course of history—policies which Juvayni had helped shape as the Ilkhanid Mongol dynasty's chief diplomat and administrator.

While Juvayni listened in silence to his courtiers, a court official brought up the question of whether or not it was permissible to eat a sea animal resembling a human, querying the experts present about the applicable dietary law. Far away in the palace corridors, cats that had stalked the merman's boat through the streets could be heard meowing loudly, as the guards tried to drive them away.

In reply to the court official, the chamberlain quoted the renowned juridical text *Qunia* which maintained that should such a human-shaped animal make speech in Arabic, and state that he is so and so, and son of such and such man, his statement should not be deemed worthy of investigation, and he should be eaten. Manifestly, the jurist who wrote *Qunia* had met a merman endowed with the power of speech who escaped his cooking pot by filling his ears with confusion and deceit. For a while everyone wondered about the lost story of *The Jurist and the Merman*, which had not come down to them, unlike the story of *Abdullah the Fisherman and Abdullah the Merman* told by storytellers in the marketplace, which gave the account of the friendship between a fisherman and a merman.

The governor sought the opinion of Qazwini, who stood on a stepladder, inspecting the merman. In addition to his accomplishments as a geographer, physician and astronomer, Qazwini was an authority on the interpretation of religious law. The final word in juristic matters at the court was reserved to him.

Qazwini stepped down and, gathering the folds of his dishevelled dark blue robe, gave a bow to the governor. Rather than offer a short reply to help him dismiss the matter as Juvayni had hoped, Qazwini launched into a discourse, based on his preliminary inspection of the merman, about the difference between the merman and the fish resembling humans described by the authors of bestiaries from antiquity to the present, dwelling upon the instances where such fish had been seen or caught, and their histories. These included the Sheikh of Sweet Speech who stole and bartered the secrets of conjugal beds; the Man of the Sea who rued offending his benefactor; Sheikh Yehudi who knew the underwater burial place of Hermes's Emerald Tablet of Magic; and the Horned Demon-Tortoise whose reincarnation was interrupted.

Juvayni knew that Qazwini did not make the lengthy preamble from a pedantic instinct or verbose impulse, but from the necessity of offering a logical argument. He listened attentively to understand why the creature had stirred his friend's curious mind.

Qazwini declared that the merman was one of Creation's marvels, which God revealed to humans so that they could reflect upon the ingenuity of His creation. To even jestingly speak about eating it was akin to making light of God's signs. Qazwini quoted Pliny the Elder from the *Naturalis Historia* that all land animals have their equivalent in the sea, and the same was true of all sea beasts. The theory seemingly encompassed humans, Qazwini commented, as validated by the merman's presence. What remained to be seen, Qazwini added, was if the diverse temperaments of the human species were also represented in their aquatic counterparts.

Qazwini offered that he would study the creature's faculties and share any further marvels he discovered in the merman. Looking keenly at Juvayni, Qazwini suggested that as the guardian of the land and the creatures which inhabited it, the governor ought to display Gujastak the Merman in his palace for all visitors to behold the manifest sign of God's handiwork.

Governor Juvayni's voice rose above the courtiers' buzz. He said if the merman were kept in the palace grounds, the few hours of quiet study left him after the court ended would also be ruined by the noise of palace guards herding and chasing spectators and idlers. The sanction to keep Gujastak the Merman at some other location was implicit in the governor's reply, however. Qazwini offered to look after arrangements for a pool to house the creature.

Despite Juvayni's discomfort at the creature's sight, he could not deny the learned man's need to study the creature. He settled with the fishermen, and commissioned one of them to stay behind as a keeper. Before the merman's boat was wheeled away, Juvayni cast another look at the creature. Oblivious to the court chatter, Gujastak lay unstirred in his boat, his only motion a twitch of the skin to drive away the flies.

THE SHEIKH OF SWEET SPEECH

A trickster called the Sheikh of Sweet Speech is a common sight on the banks of Syrian rivers. He possesses a human head and human hands and feet, but from the neck down his body is flaccid and shaped like a water buffalo's. He usually appears after sunset and saunters into city neighbourhoods. He breaks into sailors' homes when they are at sea and with his expansive gestures, cloying words, gifts of trinkets, and other such valuables convinces the women to feed and house him. He gets his name from the power he exercises over women of loose morals who open up to him with stories of their marital bed. The Sheikh carries these stories to ships and narrates them to sailors in return for valuables and trinkets after embroidering the accounts with obscene details. The Sheikh sports a beard and his face is cast in an anxious expression which disappears the moment he is in the company of women, then he becomes all mirthful and loquacious. Sometimes a woman will fall in love with the Sheikh of Sweet Speech, and he establishes himself into the household. He barks from the rooftop to announce to the neighbourhood his possession of the property and its mistress, and fights the man of the house upon his return from the sea. Being awkward in his movements, the Sheikh is easily overpowered and driven out from the house, but he is never harmed, as injuring him is supposed to bring a seven-year curse on the head of his tormentors. He is also known as the Sheikh of Whores.

—*Marvels of Things Created and*
Miraculous Aspects of Things Existing

THE MAN OF THE SEA AND HIS REGRET

The unknown manuscript of a bestiary gives the account of a creature called the Man of the Sea. He was said to be in all respects like a man, except for his oily, malodorous tail. A merchant had caught him on an island and sent him to his sovereign as a gift. Although the creature exuded a strong odour, the king found him a wonderful marvel and would not part with him. He had a seat in the court and a chair in the king's chamber. The Man of the Sea lived in the palace for many years, eating fine foods at the king's table and attending his court. With long instruction he learned the human speech. One day, the king asked him what he found most strange about human beings, upon which the Man of the Sea replied that in the merfolk the tail grows on the derriere and in the humans it grows from the chin. Since the king himself had a beard, the reply infuriated him, and he had the Man of the Sea driven out of the palace. No longer used to his natural raw diet after eating fine fare at the king's table, the Man of the Sea begged for crumbs and snatched food from people at the seashore, or raided galley kitchens on dark nights. He was known to accost galleys carrying notables and courtiers whom he would beg to intercede on his behalf with the king. However, they did not let him approach them on account of his foul odour which had grown stronger with time.

—*Marvels of Things Created and*
Miraculous Aspects of Things Existing

SHEIKH YEHUDI AND HERMES'S EMERALD TABLET

Abu Hamid al-Gharnati recorded a fish the size of a calf. Its face was human and sported a beard, but the rest of its body was shaped like a frog's. He was called Sheikh Yehudi on account of his habit of emerging from the sea on Saturday nights and staying on shore without food or drink until Sunday's sun had set, whereupon it returned to the sea. He was said to be the guardian of the Emerald Tablet that the magician Hermes Trismegistus had hidden under the sea.

Shortly after his arrival on the shore and before the moment of his return to the sea, Sheikh Yehudi made a short speech in an unknown language. It was said to contain lines from the Emerald Tablet, giving the secrets of the prima materia and its transmutation. Many an occultist and magician gathered on the seashore on Saturday night to record his speech on tablets and papyri, hoping one day to compile the entire text of the Emerald Tablet from his utterances.

The more adventurous among them dove after Sheikh Yehudi in the hope that he would guide them to the place in the sea where the Emerald Tablet was buried. None has been known to have succeeded in finding the Emerald Tablet or even keeping up with Sheikh Yehudi, a powerful swimmer.

—*Marvels of Things Created and Miraculous Aspects of Things Existing*

THE HORNED-DEMON TORTOISE AND HIS INTERRUPTED REINCARNATION

The report of a rare sighting in the waters of the Red Sea mentioned that a horned creature swimming in the sea was taken for a sea-demon until it came ashore and it was seen that from the neck down, his body was encased in a shell like a tortoise's.

According to the legend told of the creature, he was a tortoise who lived on an island. He was a confidant of the demons of the sea whom he instructed in the occult properties of plants learned from his ancestors. After the tortoise died, the demons decided to have him reincarnated as one of them as a reward for his friendship so that he could live with them in the sea.

Before taking him into the skies for the reincarnation, the sea-demons made merry over the tortoise's body, and got inebriated on rancid octopus wine in remembrance of their friend. It was a late hour, when, hoisting the dead tortoise on their shoulders, they started skywards on their journey.

Just as they were passing the sky where the dominion of the sea-demons' soul-keeper began and the tortoise's soul-keeper ended, the day ended; with only his head reincarnated into his new life as a sea-demon, the creature fell from the sky into the sea. He has a human face because all demons are given human visages in the world to allow them to mingle better with humans.

—*Marvels of Things Created and*
Miraculous Aspects of Things Existing

Chapter 3

When court ended, Qazwini went to supervise the arrangements he had ordered for housing the merman. The observatory hall located near the Shammasiyya Gate in Baghdad he had chosen to house Gujastak used to be a part of the Wisdom Chamber, a wing of the caliphal palace in Baghdad dedicated by Caliph Mamun for scholarly activities. Scholars who studied and translated the philosophical and scientific works of Greek authors into Arabic also worked there. Over time, it had expanded with the addition of an astronomical observatory, and quarters for scholars who visited Baghdad for study or research.

The burnt empty shelves and the charred murals of planetary tables were the only traces left now of the original walls. Bats had made nests in the caverns created by the fallen walls and domes. The hall was filled with dirt and the stench of cattle. The herdsmen using it as an animal pen had to be moved out, and the layers of filth covering the floor cleaned before the masons could begin constructing the pool.

Even though a year had passed since the Fall of Baghdad, Qazwini found it difficult, upon entering the ruins of the

Wisdom Chamber, to reconcile himself to its present state. There was a time when nothing could equal the sense of grandeur and scholarly purpose that prevailed in the hallowed chamber.

Qazwini had been in Baghdad on the day the city fell to the Mongols, and had seen it transform before his eyes. He had been trapped in the Wisdom Chamber when Juvayni entered the city with the first Mongol troops and set up a cordon around the building. Hearing the news of Juvayni's arrival in the city, Qazwini secretly sent him a message, requesting a meeting. Over the years, the two had met on occasion in the libraries, at debates held at the religious schools, or at assemblies at the houses of common friends. The older, more accomplished Qazwini had impressed the young, influential aristocrat with his learning and lucid discourse. In his turn Qazwini marvelled at the depth of Juvayni's knowledge of the historian's art, his powerful memory, and his ability to manoeuvre his way through intricate webs of Abbasid bureaucracy and tribal networks. They had remained in contact through the occasional correspondence on subjects of mutual interest.

At his brief meeting with Juvayni, Qazwini also met the astronomer Tusi. After his capture at Alamut by the Mongols two years earlier, the astronomer had switched allegiance, joining the Mongol court as adviser. Many had foreseen the events leading up to the Fall of Baghdad, knowing well the political weaknesses of the Abbasid dynasty and the Mongols' rapidly expanding and successful military raids. Qazwini did not blame Tusi for his change of allegiance. In fact, he was somewhat envious of Tusi's clear-headedness in the matter, and for acting swiftly to secure his interests. Eight years ago,

Qazwini had himself fled his city of birth, before a Mongol army overran it. It had disrupted his initial research for the cosmography.

At their meeting, Juvayni told Qazwini of the commands he was entrusted to carry out with Tusi's help upon Baghdad's fall. Hulagu Khan had ordered all beneficial knowledge from the Wisdom Chamber collections to be transferred to Mongol control. However, the theological commentaries, which, in Juvayni's opinion, were neither founded on tradition nor supported by reason, were to be destroyed. A similar understanding was negotiated by Juvayni with the last lord of Alamut upon Hulagu Khan's conquest of the Alamut castle in an act widely seen as the Mongols' first major acquisition of knowledge. The armillary spheres, astrolabes, and other astronomical instruments found at Alamut alongside books were now in Tusi's use.

Qazwini understood what was being asked of him by Juvayni. In a manner of speaking, he had no choice in the matter. Hulagu Khan's decree would be carried out by Juvayni and Tusi with or without his assistance. Meanwhile, if he consented to helping Juvayni with the selection of texts, he would align himself with Baghdad's future administration, and continue his research on his cosmography uninterrupted with assured access to the collection.

The town of Wasit, where Qazwini taught at the legal school, also fell after the Mongol takeover of Baghdad. At Juvayni's request Qazwini took the post of a judge in Baghdad. With no family to encumber him, his new position offered him greater influence at court and reduced responsibilities, allowing him to devote more hours to study. His escape from the monstrous flies of Wasit's marshy land was also a welcome relief.

Several theological works revered by Qazwini were destroyed during the purge of texts from the Wisdom Chamber, but his knowledge of the collection helped save many important manuscripts on the sciences with the assistance of Juvayni, Tusi, and numerous scholars and librarians held captive inside the library. Later, he saw the care and love that was lavished on the rescued texts by scholars commissioned by the Mongols, and felt relieved that the collection had given birth to another repository of knowledge. This did not take away from his grief, however, at the slaughter and destruction suffered by Baghdad at the hands of the Mongols.

Qazwini was unable to resolve a contradiction that compromised the intent of his work on his cosmography: how to reconcile his work, which sought to establish the supremacy of God's power of creation, with his act of colluding with the regime that had killed God's vicegerent. He had not changed his allegiance to the caliph so much as broken it. Every time Qazwini was beset by this conflict, he told himself that the new order was not established without the writ of God, and he should serve it under the conditions imposed upon him; that the only truth he could hold on to, and keep inviolate the belief in his faith and chosen work, was to believe that through bringing the focus on God's agency in the study of the universe and its components, his work would hopefully lay down the foundations of a new theology that would show how faith is not necessarily blind; that sensory proof, too, could offer a path to belief.

Qazwini was grateful to Juvayni for the time allowed him

to study and conduct his research, and develop his theories on the nature of existence and cosmic phenomena. Despite the horrible massacre that had taken place, and the heavy pall of gloom that even a year later enveloped the city, he was thankful for the easy access to important texts.

Chapter 4

The following day, after Qazwini had checked on Merman Gujastak, he headed for the governor's palace.

The manuscripts collected and commissioned by the Abbasid dynasty were temporarily housed in the governor's palace where they were being evaluated and re-catalogued. Qazwini walked past the guards and entered the corridor leading up to the book collection, where piles of manuscripts and papyrus rolls awaited classification by the library clerks.

A warm, dry breeze filtered into the hall through the stone-carved lattices of the library's connecting passage as Qazwini walked up to the library registrar's seat to ask about the manuscripts he wished to consult. Most of the historical texts requisitioned by Qazwini were available. The registrar suggested some other texts as well that Qazwini might find useful.

Even before occupying the desk reserved for him in the reading hall, Qazwini was formulating in his mind the preamble to introducing Gujastak in his cosmography. His ambitious scholarly labour—a text that was part cosmography and part natural history—had been underway for some time. It was designed to arouse the awe and wonder of men at the assembly of Creation—both the children of Abel, who represented the different races of humans; and the children of Cain: monsters, malformed creatures and half-beasts. He planned to do so by describing the attributes of the insects, birds and beasts; the plants and creatures of the unexplored world that lay at the depths of seas and the far reaches of the world; and the silently revolving heavens above with the angels which inhabited them.

He prided himself on his idea of organization of the cosmography; an effort amounting to a figurative conquest of the earth, the seas, and the heavens. Its contents would be listed according to the hierarchically organized universe based on the Avicennian model of creation-by-emanation, with the angels and denizens of heaven first represented, as they were closer to God in their essence. It would be a permanent tribute to the Creator's work from whom all Creation emanated, to whom it longed to return, and with whom it desired to be unified. Beyond that, Qazwini planned it to be a work that would convincingly establish divine supremacy in Creation by invoking marvel at the ordered universe, among those gifted with intellect and the power of reasoning.

Qazwini had noticed during the merman's inspection that he did not react to his touch, but exhibited a controlled alertness, revealing, what appeared to him, an almost human intelligence. Keeping in view the merman's form and size, Qazwini planned to devote himself to looking for clues about the merman among the beast-humans, whose existence could no longer be doubted.

Merman Gujastak offered Qazwini a chance for a first detailed study of a beast-human. Qazwini hoped that he might be able to form a theory of the merman's origins by comparison and analogy of the anatomy and biological mechanism of other integrated beings.

Qazwini's theory of existence defined the human as a plant by its element of development, a beast by virtue of feeling and motion, and an angel by virtue of his knowledge of the essence of things. He thought the merman could also be explained by that formulation if he changed its last words. He could define the merman as a plant by its element of development, a beast by virtue of feeling and motion, and a human by virtue of his sapience.

The study would be a crowning addition to his compendium, Qazwini felt, bringing together his many theories about the creatures, and the various stages they represented in the table of Creation.

Chapter 5

The ancient historians, Qazwini had observed, exhibited a deep curiosity about the myths and legends of the lands of which they wrote. They did not separate the present of a thing from its past, viewing history, in effect, as an organism whose phases represented different stages of its development. That was how Qazwini viewed Creation as well, which underwent incremental stages through discernible causes, rather than arbitrary changes with no known cause. Qazwini was hopeful that in the chronicles of the ancient historians he would discover the clues to what he sought. Setting his reed pens and inkwell in order, he began reading and making notes as the library clerks brought him the relevant manuscripts and papyri.

Information about the integrated beings had been recorded from the accounts and descriptions of sailors and merchants who had encountered them on distant, little known islands and faraway lands. But the encounters and sightings provided only the rudiments of their physical attributes.

There were, as well, numerous references to human-faced fruit that grew from plants and trees, such as the human-faced fruit of the waq-waq tree and others, but Qazwini did not consider them of significance to his research as their other part was a plant rather than beast. He noted the references, however, for inclusion in his cosmography as marvels of the plant species.

The Merman and the Book of Power

Chapter 6

The merman proved an absorbing subject. Qazwini began to see the difference between the beast-humans he had read about, and Merman Gujastak. In the beast-humans the animal and human properties did not breach their respective barriers: The human features were restricted to the human part of the body, and the animal features to the animal part. However, in Gujastak, canine teeth grew in a human mouth, and the reproductive organ that resembled a human male's grew on the body's fish part. Qazwini considered the possibility that the merman might turn out to be a creature in a category of his own, a being without precedent—like Kabikij, Lord of the Insects.

He also thought of the other possibility—that Gujastak was of the creatures of miraculous birth to be occasionally found among both humans and beasts. Given the singularity of such creatures, Qazwini was sceptical about discovering a general theory to define how such creatures came about; by their very nature such incidents would not fit into a theory of Creation.

Later, however, as he reflected some more on it, Qazwini

saw that Gujastak could, in fact, fit into a theory of Creation if one assumed two branches of beast-humans.

The first one was a simple beast-human comprising two or more creatures in whom the physical attributes of beast and human remained confined to their respective creature parts. Of this, the Sheikh of Sweet Speech, Sheikh Yehudi, and Man of the Sea were some examples.

The second one was a complex beast-human in whom the physical attributes breached their respective physical boundaries and showed attributes of other beings. Of that, Gujastak was the only known example.

KABIKIJ, THE SIX-LEGGED LONG-TAILED LORD OF THE INSECTS

There is a long-tailed creature called Kabikij found near the Nile where the papyrus reed grows, and in the mulberry fields in China. He has six legs and a human body. Of all creatures he is the most circumspect, always avoiding contact with humans. He is only to be seen when there is a locust attack, when he is found flying in the middle of the swarm. Despite his large size, he is difficult to differentiate in the swarm as he hides himself cleverly in their midst.

Kabikij leads the swarm with a shrill call which resembles the chirping of cicadas. He is called the Lord of Insects. He is the one who rules over insects and controls them. It is said that the letters of his name are a talisman, used as a protection against insects.

—Marvels of Things Created and
Miraculous Aspects of Things Existing

Chapter 7

In the governor's palace Qazwini awaited the arrival of a slave girl whom Juvayni had purchased while returning from a hunting expedition. The reports of her beauty, circulated by those who had seen her enter Baghdad with Juvayni's retinue, had kept the court abuzz the whole day. Qazwini was there to conduct her physical examination before she could be admitted into Juvayni's harem. He was also curious to find out the truth in the reports of her beauty. From the analysis of her urine brought to him earlier by the harem superintendent, and its rich amber colouration, he could tell she was in robust health.

As the harem superintendent led in the slave girl, Qazwini realized why everyone marvelled at her good looks. Formed of delicate features, hers was a kind of steely beauty that simultaneously displayed levity of temper and resolve of character. Despite her short and wiry frame her presence was overpowering, and her dark eyes remarkably alive and alert. There was a strange look in them when their eyes met before she lowered her gaze.

As the superintendent stared impassively, Qazwini asked the slave girl to remove all her garments and began the physical examination. He inspected the colouration of her tongue, the firmness of her teeth, the odour from her mouth, the smell of perspiration from the armpits, and the hardness of nails on her fingers and toes. As Qazwini knelt to inspect her for hemorrhoids and pubic lice, he saw a black mark that ran across the inside of her thigh in a raised, thick welt as if some beast had clawed her. Qazwini quickly looked up and saw the slave girl's face cast itself into a derisive smile. A flash of recognition brought back the memory of their last disquieting meeting so forcefully to Qazwini's mind he nearly lost his balance.

Five years ago, while Qazwini was deputed at his previous post in Wasit, he had heard stories about a beautiful, wild girl named Aydan who lived with the heathen nomads and was reputed to have great sexual prowess. She was said to have killed a young man in the act of sexual congress, having swallowed his member and scrotum with her vagina. She lived with a man who sometimes rented her out to travellers for a night or two.

Intrigued by the stories, Qazwini had bedded her after paying her master. Qazwini was not a little shocked by the wanton behaviour from one entering the first bloom of youth that she had displayed during coupling. While he felt revulsion at her loud oaths during coition, her lustful cries had excited him. Qazwini had dispersed his seed against his volition. As he withdrew in embarrassment and anxiety, she turned on him screaming. He tried to leave the tent, but she entreated him to stay, and clung to his leg, clawing and biting his member to make him rise again. When she taunted his manhood, he hit out in disgust. As she still held on to him, he violently disengaged himself, and left the tent. Qazwini's last memory of Aydan was her cursing and howling and rubbing her thighs as she rolled inconsolably on the carpet, revealing the mole shaped like a demon's claw on her inside right thigh.

Qazwini hurriedly rose from the floor and told the superintendent of the harem that the physical examination was over. He asked him to administer her immersive baths for three days in warm water of margosa leaves, and dry the body with a cloth damped in vinegar. Then he dismissed them. Aydan walked away imperiously, without casting another glance at Qazwini.

It was only after she was gone and Qazwini's breath had returned to normal that he marvelled at the transformation she had undergone from a wild creature to a stately beauty, making her unrecognizable to him when he first saw her.

Qazwini was curious if Juvayni would find Aydan of too wild a temperament to retain her.

Chapter 8

Juvayni started wearing bright coloured robes to court, and seemed distracted. A few times he dismissed the court too early with important matters pending, and rushed back to his residence, no doubt to be with Aydan.

Juvayni had a right to satisfy his desires, and Qazwini felt no attachment or association with Aydan. But Qazwini could not quite give a name to the irksome feeling he experienced at Juvayni's abandonment of his dignity and reserve.

At the court Juvayni's distracted manner grew. For a few days he invited Aydan to the court and asked her to give her opinions during consultations on official matters. Qazwini was not present during those days and felt glad about it, for he heard from those present that Aydan was insolent to officials who did not concur with her opinions. After some acrimonious exchanges between Aydan and high officials, Juvayni discontinued bringing Aydan to the court.

Qazwini saw Aydan a few times in the marketplace, travelling in state on a throne borne by slaves. She seemed perfectly happy. He saw her smiling at the passers-by, decked in finery and wearing jewels that could have only come from the Mongol treasury under Juvayni's control. She exuded a certain fragility that he did not expect to see in someone like her. Qazwini avoided her gaze, although he could feel it upon him for a few moments as she passed. He heard rumours that Juvayni was contemplating making her his wife.

Chapter 9

Qazwini's excitement at finding a principle to differentiate between the simple and complex beast-humans was short-lived. Upon further reflection he realized that there was an underlying contradiction in his formulation that presupposed such creatures as marvels of Creation. In fact, they were an incongruity; a paradox that put a question mark on man's place in the universe.

Things were easily explained if an integrated being was composed of two or more beasts. A beast-human, however, called into question the idea of human perfection as explained by faith. The creation of a beast-human was tantamount to the Creator slighting his own design. The Creator claimed that human beings were created on a perfect scheme. How could He then suggest by way of creating a beast-human that man as a creation was not paramount in cosmic order, and his corporeal boundaries were not sacrosanct and could be linked together with a beast's?

Qazwini searched for some argument that would explain the beast-humans in the Creator's scheme of existence. To understand the beast-humans as transformed creatures was one way to explain the incongruity. The holy book had mentioned earlier tribes and nations whose forms or faces deformed and became beastly on account of their deviance and wickedness. Their crimes cost them the loss of human form. The idea of the beast-humans as the continuing line of the sinful tribes did not hold up as a theory, however. The same faith which espoused the theory of human transformation into animals as punishment, also suggested that future generations were not visited with retribution for the deeds of their elders. Among the Jews and the Christians, too, the iniquity of the fathers was not visited on the children beyond the fourth generation.

Another argument to explain the existence of beast-humans lay in the history of Cain and his sister Anaq who spawned deformed creatures—the most famous being the Amorite giant, King Og of Bashan, killed by Moses and his men in the Battle of Edrei. There was the one-limbed nasnaas who had half a head, one leg, one eye, and one arm, and was born from the mating of a species of demons with humans; the gold-complexioned, chest-headed creatures who had no necks; the serpentine man with a human face and a snake-like body who was cursed to roam the earth, and such others. Qazwini wondered if the beast-humans could be the offspring of Cain and Anaq, possessing some human attributes, but also other distinguishing features that put them at variance with both beasts and humans. He could not find a logical counter to his theory. As this view was also supported by the accepted legends of the faith, it would have served him as the starting point for his larger theory had he not come upon the heretical text *The Protocols of Existence*. Its author, Khadish, had explained the nature of the universe by describing what he called its 'protocols of existence' and how they influenced events, time, and destinies.

Khadish had been put to the sword on the charge of heresy in the time of Caliph Wathiq for suggesting that more than one world was created by adversarial creators. In describing how to guard the sanctity of the human world, Khadish warned his followers to be on guard against evil infiltrating into the human world. Khadish's adherents claimed heavenly assumption for him, and revered his treatise as the text that would guide them through the years until End Time. They believed that before the end of the world Khadish would descend to lead them into battle against an Adversary from the other world.

∞

The Occultist Khadish's Protocols of Existence

If one assumed that the universe was a living organism—as Plato suggested and the animists believed—it had to be accepted as well that it was a composite organism, with each individual creature a part of its corporeal self. The nature of each individual creature—whether it be a lowly ant, or the mighty tanneen—contributed to the composite nature of the universe. From this composite nature were derived the protocols of existence to which all life in a universe conformed. All creatures within a universe were compliant to its protocols of existence as the protocols had been adapted to their natures.

The protocol of existence also served as a barrier to malign beings from other universes made by other creators. They could not breach or enter it, and if they did, they could not survive within it.

However, if a creature from another universe was somehow able to enter and survive within a universe by adoption or cunning, its individual nature would begin flowing into the universe's composite nature, adulterating it with its own. The greater the number of such alien creatures grew within a universe, the more their natures would pour into and change the composite nature of the universe, diluting and weakening its protocols of existence. In time, the protocols of existence would be sufficiently compromised to allow all kind of malignant aliens to enter and survive within it. Their spreading existence would invert the protocols altogether, and hasten its original inhabitants' exit or termination.

∞

The idea of protocols of existence and beast-humans as possible intruders from other worlds appealed to Qazwini. But he rejected Khadish's theory of multiple creators as heretical nonsense. According to Khadish since each universe had its own protocol of existence, a creature from another universe made by another creator would not survive in the human universe. As Qazwini saw it, even if the beast-humans were to be considered as intruders who did not belong in the human world, all were yet the creation of the same progenitor, and touched by His essence. Upon entering the human world the creatures would be reconciled to the human world's protocols by virtue of the divine essence that touched all His creation, for it superseded all protocols.

Qazwini remained hopeful that he would be able to resolve

the conundrum of the beast-humans' existence without doubt infiltrating the foundations of his faith. Just like reason and logic began with abstract suppositions, and arrived at truth with great perspicuity, he believed that faith helped those steadfast in it to open doors of knowledge and truth. At the moment, however, Qazwini was unable to see a clear path ahead, and returned to his notes to see if he could find a new thread of enquiry. He began with the accounts of miraculous births that he had noted earlier but had not closely studied.

Chapter 10

At first it was merely a rumour whispered in the court that Juvayni had punished Aydan for her impudence. Then it was verified that during an excursion Aydan tried in public to take liberties with Juvayni reserved for the bed, and Juvayni had whipped her.

In the coming days Qazwini looked for Aydan in the marketplace but she had stopped venturing out of the governor's palace. When Qazwini did finally see her a week later, she looked downcast and was out with an older slave woman. They were on foot. Aydan's privileges had been withdrawn, and the use of the throne proscribed her after Juvayni's censure.

Juvayni was not impulsive but could be unforgiving, even ruthless at times. Having known and experienced Aydan's feral nature, Qazwini knew that sooner or later Aydan, with her unruly manners, would cross certain bounds with Juvayni and he would discipline her. What might happen afterwards he could not tell. Qazwini could not help but feel sad when he enquired and learned from other slave girls that they had seen welts on Aydan's back.

When Qazwini next went to the court he found Juvayni

dressed in a drab brown robe. He was pensive and even sounded a little caustic. The court discipline, however, had returned to its old, efficient form.

Qazwini was able to discuss with Juvayni and get his approval for the expenses for Gujastak's pool. As the merman required a regular change of saline water, a supply chain had to be established in Basra to deliver water from the sea by mule trains in water-skins made from the skin of female sharks. The saltwater retained its properties longer, thus preserved.

Chapter 11

From reading the accounts of creatures of miraculous birth Qazwini was able to form a few broad generalizations of their nature. First, that each miraculous birth was a unique incident in a species; it was never repeated in its totality. And second, all miraculous births could be categorized as either those wherein one creature had begotten another, or those wherein the creature born was an amalgam of two or more creatures.

It was while reading about the former that Qazwini came across the account of a woman who had emerged fully formed from the belly of a fish. It was recorded by an Abbasid official, Sallam Tarjuman, who witnessed the event while travelling through the land of the Khazars.

Sallam Tarjuman narrated that he stayed in the land of Khazars for five days. On the second day he saw them catch a giant fish. They brought it ashore by making holes in its gills and tying ropes to them. As they dragged it, one of its gills swelled open, and a red-haired, pale-skinned woman came out of it. A black-and-white substance was wrapped like a lower garment from her waist to her thighs. She wept and screamed and pulled out her hair as the Khazar men led her away to their habitation. They bedded her in the belief that sexual congress with her would make their seed potent. Sallam Tarjuman learned that she died in captivity within a few days.

Chapter 12

Qazwini was interested in finding out if Sallam Tarjuman had recorded any other marvels during his journey. His initial search in the historical records for any information about the man was fruitless, but it turned up an enigmatic document from the tenth century that diverted Qazwini from his original research.

The Abbasid travel log Qazwini discovered gave an account of a mysterious creature swept overland by the Volga River over three centuries ago. The creature was described as the Commander of Gog and Magog and the Beast of the Apocalypse by the report's author, Ahmad ibn Fadlan, a scholar of Islamic jurisprudence. He had left Baghdad on 21 June 921 with an embassy from the Abbasid caliph Muqtadir to King Almış Iltäbär of the Volga Bulgars.

Ibn Fadlan's account comprised official reports of travels undertaken, expenses incurred, and details of the routes followed. The purported purpose of ibn Fadlan's mission was to guide King Almış Iltäbär, recently converted to Islam, in Islamic religious code. The embassy was sent at the king's request; he sought a military pact with the Abbasids, and their help in constructing defenses against his enemies, the Khazars. But the details of the Commander of Gog and Magog and his mysterious death made up the greater part of the account.

Qazwini made a copy of the entry from ibn Fadlan's record, put away the manuscript, and left a note for the clerks to remove it from his desk.

IBN FADLAN'S ACCOUNT OF THE
COMMANDER OF
GOG AND MAGOG

After a journey of two thousand and five hundred miles, we reached King Almış Iltäbär's capital on 12 May 922.

Our initial reception was lukewarm when the king discovered that the caliph had not sent the gold requested for the construction of the fortress. He was mollified, however, when the accompanying Abbasid commanders held out the promise of a military pact from the caliph. While the officials discussed military matters, I broached the subject of the Creature of the Apocalypse whose reports had reached Baghdad. King Almış Iltäbär told me that the Beast of the Apocalypse prophesied by St John had been washed ashore by the stormy Volga during the reign of the then king and his grand-uncle. When the king rode out to witness the marvel, he beheld one from the race of giants measuring twelve cubits, whose legs were covered with fish-scales. His head was like a cauldron, his eyes huge, and his nose and fingers the size of the human arm. The king brought him to his court, and sent out enquiries about him to the sovereigns and chiefs of the neighbouring lands. One of them confirmed that the creature was the Commander of Gog and Magog, who had escaped from an opening in Alexander's Rampart.

After a few months, an emissary in a green robe from a faraway land arrived by sea and expressed a desire to see the creature. Until that day the giant had never spoken, and everyone was astonished when the green-robed emissary conversed with the giant in a language he understood. The emissary left after a few days, and two months afterwards the creature died. He was still displayed in the enclosure outside the palace where he had been kept.

I asked and was shown the remains of the Commander of Gog and Magog, whose body was now covered by moss, shrubbery grew from his mouth, and his shrunken hands and feet were ossified. Such are the Creator's marvels, and the signs with which he sends warnings. May the evil attracted to inscribed words and graven images be always thwarted, and perish in like manner.

Chapter 13

Qazwini could only wonder what the embassy from Muqtadir's court made of the death of the beast from River Volga. The Beast prophesied by St John was known as the Beast of the Earth in Islamic eschatology, although this behemoth-like chimerical creature was described differently by different writers. These reports were often confused with reports of the evil giant Dajjal, the Antichrist or the Demon of Destruction, who was believed to have been hiding on an island, awaiting the announcement of his advent.

Another beast believed by some authorities to be the Dajjal was the legendary tanneen, mythical in his manifestation, legend, and power, who was first recorded by the Israelites. None had seen him in recent memory, although many merchant ships delayed at sea because of storms blamed the tanneen's motion underwater where, it was believed, he bided his time.

THE BEAST OF THE EARTH AND HIS DOINGS

The Beast of the Earth would appear before End Time one afternoon when the sun had risen from the west. He would speak to humans, and mark the believers with the staff of Moses, and the unbelievers with the seal of Solomon. He would have the head of an elephant, the horns of a stag, the eyes of a swine, the neck of an ostrich, the chest of a lion, the colouration of a tiger, the tail of a ram, the haunches of a cat, and the legs of a camel, and he would have a distance of twelve cubits between each pair of his joints.

—*Marvels of Things Created and Miraculous Aspects of Things Existing*

DAJJAL, THE DEMON OF DESTRUCTION

There is an island called Jassasa which is named after the creature who carries news to Dajjal, the Antichrist.

The narrator Tamim al-Dari reported that he sailed in a ship in the Red Sea with thirty men of Lakham and Judhaam and they were tossed by the waves of the sea for a month. One day, as the sun was setting, they came to an island that was avoided by the sailors.

It was said that those who travelled by the island in the mornings heard sweet songs, and those who travelled past the island in the evening heard terrifying screams. Having no food or water they had no choice but to disembark and search for nourishment. They sat in a small rowing boat and reached the island, which they discovered abounding in fruits and fresh water. As they sat down to rest they were met by a hirsute beast whose face was indistinguishable from his back, and they thought he was the devil. They asked the beast who he was, whereupon he answered that he was Jassasa, and pointed to a cave and said that his master was keen to know about them.

When the sailors arrived at the cave they found a giant who was bound strongly in chains with his hands tied to his neck and his legs clamped in iron shackles from the knees to the ankles. They asked him who he was whereupon the giant replied that they would soon find out about him. Then the giant asked them about the date-palm trees of Baysaan and enquired if they still bore fruit. When they answered that the date-palm trees of Baysaan still bore fruit, the giant replied that soon they would not bear fruit. Then he asked them about the lake of Tabariyyah and enquired if there was water in it. They replied that there was a great deal of water in it, upon which he replied that soon it would dry up. Then he asked them about the spring of Zughar in Syria and enquired if there was water in the spring and if the people grew crops with the water of the spring. They answered that there was plenty of water in it and the people grew crops with it, upon which the giant replied that soon there would be no water and no crops would grow. Then he announced to them that he was Dajjal the Antichrist, and that he would emerge soon into the world. He would travel on land and his wrath would not spare any town except the two holy cities guarded by angels with swords.

—*Marvels of Things Created and*
Miraculous Aspects of Things Existing

THE MONSTER TANNEEN, HIS DEEDS AND ORIGINS

The tanneen is a terrifying, gargantuan beast who is two parsang long; his breadth corresponds to his large size. He has the colouration of a panther and his body is covered with scales. He has two large arms, and his head that resembles the human face is the size of a hillock. Six snake-heads, each measuring twenty yards, are appended to his neck. He has two small ears and two large, flashing, rounded eyes. He is large-toothed, and the expanse of his maw is great enough to be able to swallow large marine animals whole.

Once this beast's stomach is full he raises his belly above water in an arch and exposes it to the sun, which helps him digest his food. His movement underwater causes turmoil and engenders sea waves.

It is related that the tanneen was once mentioned in the assembly of the scholar Amar al-Bakkali and he asked if anyone knew his origins and whence he came. When everyone expressed their ignorance he narrated that he was a dragon that had caused havoc among the land animals whom he had devoured in great numbers. The land animals pleaded with God for relief. He took pity on them, and at His order two angels carried the tanneen and threw him into the sea. The tanneen did not mend his ways even in the sea where he caused much anguish among the marine animals by gorging on their tribe.

Then the sea animals pleaded to God who again sent the angels to help. They pulled the tanneen out of the sea and hoisted him into the clouds moving towards the lands of Gog and Magog.

The cloud dropped the tanneen there and the ravenous hordes of Gog and Magog ate him up. But others of his race still lurk under deep water.

From that day God has appointed a cloud over their race. It pulls him out of the sea, in much the same manner as a magnet pulls iron filings. It is the fear of this cloud that keeps the tanneen underwater. He does not dare to show his face above the surface until he is satisfied that the skies are clear.

It is said that once upon a time the cloud lifted a tanneen out of the waters of Antioch. As it carried him away, the tail of the beast struck against the fortifications of the city, and nineteen towers of Antioch Fort collapsed from the impact.

Hippocrates narrated that a plague of foul air inundated the cities by the sea where he lived and it was discovered that the clouds had dropped the body of a tanneen two hundred parsang from the seashore; its stench had befouled the air. The citizens pooled together money to buy salt to pour over the tanneen from ships which reduced the power of the fetor.

Some heretical scholars alluded to the tanneen as an analogy for Dajjal the Demon of Destruction. They suggested that his hideous form was the dark cave in which he was imprisoned, and his six heads were its six spies, each one of them keeping an eye on one of the six directions, and each knowing the speech of one of the six species: bird, beast, fish, man, jinn, and angel. It was on this account that he remained alert and knowledgeable about what passed in the world and the heavens.

—*Marvels of Things Created and*
Miraculous Aspects of Things Existing

Chapter 14

Qazwini had decided to incorporate ibn Fadlan's account of the sea creature from the Volga River in his entry for the merman. But while rereading his copy of the account, his mind got stuck on the circumstances and timing of ibn Fadlan's embassy.

He recalled that shortly before the time ibn Fadlan's embassy departed, Baghdad had mourned the heavy loss of lives suffered by the Abbasid army in battle against the Greeks. Thousands of young, male Abbasid subjects had been taken prisoner and sold in the slave markets of Asia. The caliphate had lost North Africa as a dominion. Rebellions kept breaking out between the Mamluk groups holding power in Baghdad, keeping the caliphate in constant turmoil. The Abbasid subjects blamed the events on Caliph Muqtadir's dereliction of duties. The citizens had protested the proclamation of Muqtadir's name—whose corrupt ways were proverbial—during the Friday sermons by stoning the prayer leaders, but that too had failed to elicit a response from him. The caliph had received a gift of twenty Byzantine slave girls of exquisite beauty after the recently concluded armistice with the Byzantine Empress, and new advancements in music theory under the philosopher and musicologist Farabi had improved the quality of musical offerings at the court. The caliph was happy in his diversions, and oblivious to the political and strategic crises building around him.

King Almış Iltäbär of Volga Bulgars had likely not detected the decline of the caliphate's power. He could be forgiven for imagining that a pact with the Abbasids would deter his enemies from invading his lands. Caliph Muqtadir's response, however, was uncharacteristic of the man. Why should someone of Muqtadir's disposition care about a faraway, insignificant land and send a caliphal embassy at some expense in order to deliver guidance in the religious code? Such a step could not have been taken without a consensus at court, as the caliph was little more than a puppet in the hands of powerful courtiers. What cause could have brought together the voluptuaries, conspirators and mercenaries wielding power at Caliph Muqtadir's court to support the mission? There was something amiss in ibn Fadlan's account.

Qazwini realized that ibn Fadlan seemed to give the creature more weight than the military pact and religious instruction, the visit's purported reason. Could it be that investigating and confirming the appearance of the Commander of Gog and Magog—news of which had reached Baghdad according to ibn Fadlan—was the main reason for the embassy? But how was the monster's appearance in the Volga River connected to the powers in Baghdad? Was it the caliph's fear of the Beast of End Time that made him send the embassy? Ibn Fadlan's last words about evil being attracted to inscribed words and graven images were cryptic and seemed to hint at some unknown anticipations about the creature. He sounded relieved at the creature's death.

There was the question, too, about the green-robed emissary who had spoken to the beast in the creature's own language before ibn Fadlan's visited there. Who was he? Which power did he represent? What was the subject of their conversation with the commander of Gog and Magog?

When Qazwini tried to locate the records from Caliph Muqtadir's era when ibn Fadlan's embassy was sent, he learned that they were sent to Azerbaijan. The astronomer Tusi had convinced Hulagu Khan to finance the Rasadkhana observatory in Azerbaijan to develop his work on the tables of the planetary movements. With him he had taken a smaller portion of the Wisdom Chamber collection comprising four hundred thousand manuscripts and a part of the record of the Abbasid court. Qazwini wrote to Tusi requesting copies of the records he needed to consult. He felt the circumstances and reasons for ibn Fadlan's embassy would remain draped in a veil of mystery unless they were closely studied.

Chapter 15

After making his daily observations of Gujastak, and inspecting to ensure that the pool's construction proceeded at a satisfactory pace, Qazwini headed to the court to carry out his duties as a judge.

The crimes committed by the citizens of Baghdad before the Mongol invasion and during the fall of the city were still being investigated and brought to account.

A case was brought forward by a man whose daughter was kidnapped and sold by his neighbour to slavers who had followed Hulagu Khan's forces to Baghdad. The aggrieved father had traced his daughter to a household in Mosul, and requested the Mongol court to recover her and punish the person responsible for the deed. The acts committed by the Mongols during the attack on Baghdad were inviolable but Qazwini ruled in favour of the plaintiff, reasoning that the case involved a conspiracy by a caliphal subject in connivance with the slavers to blame Mongol soldiers.

Having dispensed with the decisions and judgments due on that day, ordered further investigations where circumstances warranted, and finished processing witness accounts, Qazwini made a visit to the marketplace to purchase some herbs whose healing properties he wished to describe in his cosmography.

When Qazwini returned after sunset, he found Gujastak restive. He restlessly struck with his tail the inside of the boat and tried to climb over its bow. The guard tried to force him back into the boat but the keeper stopped him. Once perched atop the bow, Gujastak turned his head around and looked past Qazwini to the hall's back entrance. Following his gaze, Qazwini saw a man clad in a dark robe standing there.

Qazwini ordered one of the guards to question the man. But by the time the guard reached the back entrance, the man was gone, swallowed by the network of dark alleys into which the entrance led. Qazwini imagined it was someone curious about the merman, and gave it no further thought. He had finished Gujastak's observations for the day. Before he left, he cast a last glance at the merman who was slowly lowering himself back into the boat, using his hands and arms as support.

Chapter 16

Baghdad was not new to outlandish rumours, but Qazwini was disturbed to hear it being whispered in the marketplace that Gujastak was the Agent of the Apocalypse, the portent of some great destruction to come. Qazwini found it curious for Gujastak to be described as a creature connected to the apocalypse, much like the one he was researching in an effort to trace the merman's antecedents.

The development was disturbing for another reason, too. Rumours about an impending apocalypse had been heard when Hulagu Khan's armies were advancing on Baghdad. People imagined them as the hordes of End Time creatures Gog and Magog. The fall of the divinely sanctioned caliphate to the Mongols was in many ways an unimaginable catastrophe; why many in Baghdad interpreted it as an apocalyptic event. Anything associated with the apocalypse, therefore, brought back memories which had left a deep and festering imprint on the people's imaginations, and for that reason Qazwini found it worrisome for Gujastak to be associated with its symbols.

Disquieted as he was by the development, Qazwini dismissed it, thinking that the rumour would die in due course.

The rumour only gained strength, however, and one afternoon Qazwini rushed to the hall after receiving news that a violent crowd carrying stones had gathered outside Gujastak's hall. When Qazwini arrived there he found the hall surrounded. He heard the crowd call Gujastak the devil's child. The old man leading them looked familiar, although Qazwini could not see his face clearly in the pressing crowd. A strange madness seemed to have gripped those gathered there, and they refused to listen to Qazwini's pleas to disperse peaceably. He was pushed aside as the crowd pelted stones and tried to storm the hall. Were it not for the timely charge by the troopers who dispersed them with the flats of their swords and horsewhips, the frenzied crowd may have succeeded in overpowering Gujastak's guard and keeper and harmed him.

Throughout the commotion Gujastak sat in his boat, combing his hair with his long fingers. He remained deaf to the voices seeking him, and the subsequent stampede and cries as the troopers scattered the crowd.

The man leading the mob had been arrested. Despite his greatly changed looks, Qazwini recognized Duraid, one of the Wisdom Chamber's former librarians, when he was produced before him. Qazwini was seeing him for the first time in almost a year. His ancestors had worked in the library since its founding during the reign of Caliph Mamun. When the Mongols besieged the library, Duraid's only son, who also worked as a clerk at the library, was outdoors. As Duraid helped Qazwini and others to save books from the collection, his son tried to reach the Wisdom Chamber for news of his father, and was killed in the massacre. After the captive librarians were given their freedom by Juvayni, and invited to continue working under the Mongols, Duraid did not return.

Duraid refused to answer Qazwini's queries about his role in inciting the crowd, nor gave any reasons for his actions. Qazwini had no desire to detain the old man, or send him to a dungeon where someone in his state of health would hardly survive a few days. Qazwini dismissed him with a warning not to incite trouble again. Duraid seemed a little surprised at Qazwini's lenience and his acquittal. He stood pensively for a few moments, then said without looking at Qazwini that it was the sign of End Time when evil manifested itself in the form of strange beasts visiting humans. He added that the Mongols would be annihilated in the same manner as the Abbasids, and the Byzantines before them.

That Duraid saw the merman as a manifestation of some evil associated with End Time was obvious, but he either did not know the evil's nature himself, or would not tell Qazwini. As Duraid turned and walked away, feeling the walls of the dimly lit hall with his hands, Qazwini noticed how frail he had become.

In people's minds Gujastak's association with End Time creatures or events had manifested in trouble, as Qazwini had feared. He ordered another armed guard deputed at the entrance to the hall to prevent similar incidents in the future, and had it announced in the marketplace that any further attacks on the merman would be dealt with severely.

The incident provoked by Duraid, and his words, continued to trouble Qazwini. He wondered if Duraid's mental faculties were compromised by the shock of the violent death of his son, for his mind seemed to be clouded: while the Mongols had been victorious over the Abbasids, the latter had not vanquished the Byzantine Empire, as Duraid had seemed to imply. The old librarian's words had reminded Qazwini of how ibn Fadlan, too, referred to the creature as a portent, an omen, and harbinger of future events.

Chapter 17

Gujastak had finally been moved into the newly constructed pool made with jet stone, granite and alabaster. Qazwini had supervised the move and felt that he seemed well-settled.

The pool was cleaned every five days. Gujastak sat atop the ledge of the raised pool and surveyed the hall as the labourers drained it out, and scraped algae off the walls. Sometimes he made threatening sounds in his incomprehensible aquatic babble resembling the bark of carrion-eaters. As the workers cursed him back, he bared his fangs and laughed, his large, translucent belly shaking. Once the men had finished with their task and the pool was refilled, he lunged and disappeared into it with a swish of his heavy tail. A burble of what sounded like abuse rang out from the pool's bottom, bursting in bubbles upon the surface from his exhalations.

Qazwini, meanwhile, planned for the future. He had acquired Juvayni's permission to have the adjoining hall repaired and cleaned, where he contemplated the construction of a bigger pool. Dispatches were sent to agents at seaports and navarchs of outgoing vessels, asking for news of any sightings or capture of merwomen. For centuries there had been reports of large-breasted merwomen with capacious vaginas, who sang irresistible songs to sailors, promising them carnal bliss. They addled the sailors' brains with overpowering desire; sailors would then bring them onboard to lie with them. The merwomen dragged the sailors underwater with the promise of greater pleasures that awaited them, only to feast on them with their sharp teeth.

Fishermen who caught them in their nets sold them at a good price to sailors whose companions had been lured and killed by merwomen. They avenged the death of their friends and companions by quenching their lust upon them in cruel ways, before cooking them alive on the spit and eating them. Qazwini hoped that regardless of the merwomen's activities in the sea, they would prove harmless in captivity, and if perchance one were caught, she could be brought to Baghdad for Gujastak to start a family.

Chapter 18

In his weekly report Juvayni had notified Hulagu Khan about Gujastak. A deeply superstitious person, Hulagu Khan in his reply demanded to know more about the creature, and what omen his manifestation portended. Juvayni delegated to Qazwini the task of keeping Hulagu Khan abreast of all news pertaining to the creature.

Thereafter, along with the weekly dispatch from Baghdad sent to Hulagu Khan's headquarters in Maragha under the governor's seal, a chronicle of Gujastak's life was also forwarded to him.

With the reports of the flooding in Tigris, the arrival of the embassy from Byzantium, and the first wheat crop planted by the Mongols in Iraq, Hulagu Khan learned that Gujastak had taken to plaiting his hair in mimicry of his Mongol guards and made motions as if he were riding a horse, swimming upright in the pool.

The intelligence Juvayni sent Hulagu Khan a week later contained details of the Mamluks' raids on his border outposts, and a request to send one of his court storytellers to Baghdad to help corroborate a few historic details for his universal history. Qazwini's report, accompanying the governor's missive, narrated how Gujastak baited and caught two large tomcats. The pair had stalked him since his arrival in Baghdad. Gujastak chewed them alive after first biting off their heads, and later pleated their tails in his hair, displaying them as trophies.

In the interim Qazwini had heard from Tusi in Azerbaijan. He had written about the progress he had made in his work on the observatory, enquired about the work that presently occupied Qazwini, and informed him that copies of the records requested by him were being made and will soon be dispatched.

Chapter 19

Qazwini felt that an explanation for the beast-humans' presence in the human world should also answer why strange beasts were seen as signs of impending destruction by people through the ages. He wanted to probe the equation between a creature made of flesh, blood and bones, and the time and events it influenced. How did a creature become a portent? Who or what made him so? How did a being control and fashion the destiny of an individual or a people?

Certain forms of augury used animals for divining the future. Each of the different tribes in both the Umayyad and Abbasid armies had their traditional method of augury. Haruspicy involved the inspection of the entrails of animals where deities planted omens. Hepatoscopy studied their liver. The Mongols swore by scapulimancy, the science of reading the anima's shoulder blades to foretell the future. But a living creature influencing the fate of humans or a society was a phenomenon without precedent. Yet, ibn Fadlan's account was proof that a creature had been awaited and investigated over a century by those who associated it with apocalyptic events. More recently, there was Merman Gujastak. Yet Qazwini had found nothing in the history of ideas or the canonical literature of faith that satisfactorily answered such phenomena.

The Merman and the Book of Power

Chapter 20

Recourse to logic and reason had always helped Qazwini in his work as cosmographer, but it had never forced him to search for meaning outside the confines of his belief. Investigating the nature of the beast-humans, however, Qazwini found himself revisiting Khadish's theory of adversarial creators.

Reason forced the consideration that if the beast-humans could not be explained within the framework of faith, perhaps he should look for an answer outside it. Could beast-humans be the work of another creator as Khadish claimed? It meant more than one power existing independently in the universe. As a sovereign power the other power would have to be considered adversarial. And since faith stated that all opposition to the Creator came from Satan, the Adversary would have to be considered unholy.

Qazwini's faith allowed the Adversary certain powers to influence events in the human world through wile and deceit, but not the power of creation. To Qazwini, the implications of a second creator in the universe were profound. The Avicennian doctrine of creation-by-emanation allowed for multiple worlds as long as they all had the same Creator. If the existence of another creator were to be believed, it destroyed the doctrine's universality. It imperilled the entire philosophical framework and the edifice of faith Qazwini had used to explain and categorize Creation in his cosmography.

If the existence of the beast-humans proved the Adversary's power of creation, it suggested other things, too. By its nature the power of creation was without bounds and limits, and invested with such power, the Adversary may well have created an entire universe to which the beast-humans could belong.

Chapter 21

Khadish had only explained that a creature from another universe could enter and survive within the human universe by adoption or cunning. Qazwini wished to understand how their natures adapted themselves to another world's protocols.

It was reasonable to think that a creature would face resistance from the other world's protocols in direct proportion to its convolution. If a highly complex life form such as a human being, equipped with both intelligence and free will, attempted to infiltrate another universe, each of his several faculties would have to contend with and adjust to the attributes of the other world's protocols, making the adaptation difficult, if not impossible. A less complex life form, such as a beast or a bird, which did not possess intelligence and free will, would fare better against another world's protocols. And a plant that was the least complex life form, possessing neither intelligence, nor organs, would face the least resistance and adpt soonest to the other universe's protocols.

Qazwini imagined the same would hold true for creatures from other worlds trying to invade the human world: it would be practicable to first infiltrate the human world in plant form.

Once they had acclimatized, and adapted to the protocols of the human world, they could slowly start burgeoning into more complex life forms.

The human world already offered an example from this principle of life, he realized. Aristotle in his *History of Animals* had written that the fruits of the wild fig contained wasps that were spontaneously generated and upon reaching full adulthood split their skin and flew out of the fig. Qazwini also recalled several references to plant-humans he had seen earlier in the texts he had consulted and which still awaited reading and classification by him for his cosmography.

THE MAN-SHAPED FRUIT OF THE TREE ON MAMKUB ISLAND

The seas are full of islands reserved by God for his many creatures. Some of these islands are in the possession of humans, others in the control of the jinn, and yet others inhabited by birds and beasts of fantastic varieties and other living things that are neither fully plant, nor fully beast, nor fully human.

A tree which grows on the island of Mamkub is among such creatures. Its fruit is shaped like a man. After it appears on the tree, a gourd-like form with two teats appears beside it. The human-shaped fruit nurses itself on the milk of that gourd, and grows up to three cubits in length.

After attaining that length it begins to shrivel and dry. Once it has completely dried, it falls from the tree and another fruit appears on the tree-bough.

The dried fruit seems to decay fast on the ground as it is seldom found under the tree except, sometimes, in the uninhabited network of tunnels that surround the tree trunk. No animal is ever seen going in or coming out of those tunnels, and it is not known how long they stretch, and to what they connect. No other trees of its kind grow around it suggesting that its fruit does not carry its seed, and it is the only tree of its kind.

—*Marvels of Things Created and Miraculous Aspects of Things Existing*

THE WOMAN-SHAPED FRUIT OF THE
TREE IN QARIA-E NASIRA

There is an island called Qaria-e Nasira in the inhabited quarter of the world. A tree grows there that bears a citrous fruit shaped like a woman. This fruit has two arms, two legs, a pair of breasts, and a vagina. When a sailor happens to pass by, the woman-shaped fruit asks him a riddle. If the sailor is able to answer the riddle, the fruit falls to the ground as a beautiful woman and goes away with the sailor, but if he answers the riddle incorrectly, a noose of dry vines falls around the sailor's neck from the tree and pulls him up until he is hanging lifeless.

It is for this reason that sailors often converse with the tree not alone but in a group. They are able to come to the help of their companions before the noose tightens around their necks. Sometimes deadly fights break out between sailors over the rights of possession of the woman from the tree if they have answered the riddle correctly. It is for this reason that despite risks to their lives, some sailors prefer to answer the riddle by themselves.

—*Marvels of Things Created and*
Miraculous Aspects of Things Existing

THE WAQ-WAQ TREE OF INDIA

The isle of Waq-Waq in the Indian Ocean gets its name from the waq-waq tree that grows there. Its fruit is shaped in the exact likeness of a human. Although it shows signs of life through its movement, it does not speak. Only the movement of wind through the tree leaves produces the sound 'waq-waq'.

The flesh of its fruit is appetizing, and it is said that the waq-waq tree is a remnant of the crop that was the staple of jinn on Earth before the Age of Adam. It made the waq-waq sound to announce the ripening of the fruit to the jinn. It was only after Adam received the status of the Most Noble Creature that the eating of this fruit was proscribed for the jinn as a sign of respect to the shape of human beings. After the advent of Islam the jinn's diet was restricted to just dung and bones. That is the reason why the jinn hold humans in disdain, look upon them as enemies, and help the devs hunt and eat them.

—Marvels of Things Created and
Miraculous Aspects of Things Existing

THE HUMAN-SHAPED FRUIT OF THE TREE OF YOUTH

The King of Talitaka has a tree in his royal garden which once a year bears fruit shaped like humans. If one year the fruit is shaped like a man, the following year it is shaped like a woman.

While their faces and mouth are fully formed, these fruit do not speak. However, when plucked, the man-shaped fruit makes a resonant buzzing sound like a cicada's, and the woman-shaped fruit make a shrill call resembling an osprey's. It is said that these sounds are their death rattle.

The fruit of this tree are bestowed upon the favourites of the king. These have the property that if an old woman or man were to eat the fruit of their sex, they would overnight become youthful in appearance. It is for this reason that the King of Talitaka and his harem are all pictures of youth, and his court is full of fresh-faced men and women.

—*Marvels of Things Created and
Miraculous Aspects of Things Existing*

Chapter 22

Qazwini reckoned that if Khadish's theory was true, and the beast-humans were the foot soldiers of the Adversary, they would be able to navigate the human cosmos and survive within it because they conformed to its protocols as part humans. It was inevitable that, in time, other malignant creatures, too, should find their way to the human world.

All creatures, such as the man-eating manticore, which displayed in its being the parts of three creatures, with a human head surmounting a lion's body appendaged by a scorpion's tail that shot arrows; the dog-headed man-eating creatures sailors and merchants had encountered; the thong-legged men who overpowered and killed their victims by choking their windpipes; and the sea-assassin Zityron who nursed an unknown vendetta against seafaring men, might have been the Adversary's vanguard, guided into the human cosmos by his hand and machinations, and busy implementing his agenda.

MANTICORE, THE EATER OF MEN AND SOULS

In his *Memoirs*, Damis, the disciple of the occultist and sorcerer Apollonius of Tyana wrote the following regarding the creature known as manticore:

My master—may his memory be venerated—told us that the creature manticore had made allegiance of submission to humans in whose memory he was marked with the ring of dark hair encircling his neck. Later, falling prey to the council of the Adversary, and poisoned by the thorn of rebellion he implanted in his heart, the manticore turned against man, swearing death and destruction upon him. He came to be known as *murday-khor* or 'the eater of man', from which term his name is derived. He has a leonine body surmounted by a human head; while his tail is a veritable quiver of poisonous quills, each a cubit long and sharp as needle, which he shoots at those who try to subdue or kill him.

Only the yogis of India—in whose land he is found—know how to capture and tame him by baiting him with human corpses, which they make animated by transferring their souls into them. Once the manticore has consumed the corpse, the yogi's soul finds admission inside the manticore, and subdues him by removing the thorn of rebellion from his heart.

The yogis ride the manticores to the heavens to listen to the whisperings of the angels, for like the griffin the manticore, too, is an indefatigable flyer, and versed in the ways of the heavens.

—*Marvels of Things Created and*
Miraculous Aspects of Things Existing

THE DOG-HEADED MAN-EATERS

There is an island named Sagsar, or the Land of the Dog-headed, the details of which were recorded by Yaqub ibn Ishaq Siraj from the account of a sailor who had landed there.

The witness narrated that he was adrift in his boat in rough seas when strong winds drove him to a far-off island. When he disembarked there he met a group of dog-headed creatures with human bodies. Their group surrounded him and one of them stepped out and with a stick drove him like a goat to a house where he found other captive humans, and he, too, entered captivity alongside them.

The creatures daily fed them wild fruit. A man imprisoned there warned him that they were being fed so that they could put on weight and then one after another they would be roasted and eaten by the dog-headed creatures. Upon hearing this the sailor drastically reduced his diet. In the meanwhile, his companions who had become fat were eaten by the dog-headed creatures. As he had become weak from reducing his food intake, the creatures released him in the island to eat freely what he wished. The man who had first warned him about the man-eaters had also survived because he too had become very weak and sickly from curtailing his diet. He told the sailor that the dog-headed creatures celebrated a festival for which they travelled to a far-off destination where they stayed for three days. He advised the sailor to use the opportunity to escape from there, as he himself was unable and too sickly to join him. He told him that the dog-headed creatures were fleet footed and could pick up the human scent from leagues away, but if one wished to escape them one should take refuge under a black tree that grew in the far recesses of the island, and anyone who could reach its shade was safe from them.

The sailor who already had freedom to roam the island set out on the eve of the festival and kept running for one night and one day. The dog-headed creatures learned of his escape. They raised a great racket with their howling and barking as they gave him chase. Just when they were yelping at his heels and about to bring him down, the sailor managed to reach the black tree. The dog-headed creatures turned back, growling angrily, as they seemed to be afraid of something in the tree or repelled by the smell of its flowers, and the sailor was finally rid of them and found a passing barge to carry him to safety.

—Marvels of Things Created and
Miraculous Aspects of Things Existing

THE THONG-LEGGED MAN-EATERS

The chronicler Yaqub ibn Ishaq Siraj had recounted the account of another sailor on the same island whose boat capsized close to the Sagsar Island one night.

The sailor made it to the shore in the darkness and spent the next day exploring the island. He saw a group of fair-looking people gathered under a fruit-laden tree and went towards them. He sat beside them but could not understand their language, and they too found his speech incomprehensible.

While he was sitting there one of them grabbed his neck and climbed onto his shoulders. He wrapped his legs around him, and only then did the sailor realize that while these creatures looked human, they had no bones in their legs and could not walk. The creature who had climbed onto his shoulders goaded him to run. The sailor tried to dislodge him but the creature gave him powerful blows on his face and he found it impossible to get rid of him. The thong-legged creature made the sailor carry him under fruit-laden trees. He would pick and eat the fruits and share them with his fellow creatures, who would all laugh and make merry.

It so happened that the thong-legged creature's face struck a protruding tree branch which blinded him in both eyes. The sailor took advantage of his blindness to squeeze grapes and give their juice to his captor who became drunk on them until his grip on the sailor's neck and shoulders loosened. The sailor dislodged him and escaped his clutches.

Yaqub ibn Ishaq Siraj, who recorded the sailor's account, witnessed that his face was scratched from the creature slapping him with his claws.

—*Marvels of Things Created and
Miraculous Aspects of Things Existing*

THE SEA-ASSASSIN ZITYRON

The poet Yaqub Maerlanti described it as a creature whose lower body ended in a finned tail resembling a fish's, but it had the head of a man, and called it the Warrior of the Sea.

A Byzantine captain's nautical tract recorded that he and his shipmates encountered and killed the creature Zityron in the Caspian Sea when it jumped into their boat one night crying loudly, and attacked him and his companions.

According to the captain, the creature which attacked them matched Yaqub Maerlanti's description. It had hard but flexible arms with which it struck, and two fingers in each hand with which it tried to throttle them. It fought them standing on the floor of their vessel upon the tip of its tail. An armour of hard bone growing around its body deflected their blades. In the end he and his companions killed the Zityron with blows from their heavy oars and hammers. There are many accounts of this species attacking humans unprovoked, and none know the reason for the vendetta they carry out against humans.

—*Marvels of Things Created and*
Miraculous Aspects of Things Existing

Chapter 23

Qazwini asked himself if the presence of the beast-humans in the human world was the Adversary's attempt to demonstrate that he exercised power within the Creator's universe? Did the beast-humans invade the human world to conquer it? Did they do so to eclipse man—the pride of Creation—and his world with their pollution?

The defences of the human world would continue to weaken as the Adversary's numbers multiplied. The manifestation of a complex beast-human like Gujastak who had no parts that were fully human or fully beast-like, proved that the Adversary's creatures continued to evolve into more complex life forms as well. It could be interpreted from it that the protocols had deteriorated even further; that the Adversary could now send in his myrmidons.

The prospect of human world slowly headed towards destruction recalled to Qazwini's mind the rupture in the Rampart that would allow Gog and Magog to invade and overrun human dominions. The appearance of strange creatures and beasts was indeed an ill omen, as the old librarian Duraid's comments suggested, because it meant the inner defences of the world had succumbed to unholy forces. The history and events Qazwini had studied thus far made it clear that such omens were well understood by different groups of people from a very early time.

He felt that the analogy of Gog and Magog could also fit many other events from history when the terror of invasion and conquest were let loose upon a society whose inner defenses had been compromised. Both Dajjal the Demon of Destruction and the Messiah who redeemed the world could merely be symbols with changing faces that marked the fortunes of human world, and the apocalyptic events in every age.

Chapter 24

Hulagu Khan's obsession with the pharaohs—the world's first monarchs—had grown since one had appeared to him in a dream, bidding him to retrieve from the pyramids what was his by rights as the world's new imperator. He was convinced that some prophesy linking his name to the Mongols' rise would be found in the ancient texts buried in the pyramids. He had sent a number of spies into Egypt to break into the pyramids and retrieve the pharaonic texts. After several unsuccessful attempts, one spy had finally returned to Baghdad from Egypt with a preserved papyrus with script. Juvayni sent Hulagu Khan the expedition's chronicle along with the papyrus which nobody had been able to decode.

The dispatch included a letter from Qazwini which spoke of his excitement, based on his observations, upon discovering empathy and intelligence in Gujastak.

Gujastak had shown a preference for raw flesh over cooked meat. The palace butcher daily emptied bones, sinews and viscera into the trough attached to the pool. One day, during Gujastak's feeding time, a cat that had wandered in unnoticed jumped onto the pool's ledge, close to the merman. Gujastak looked alert to the cat's presence, and watched her from the corner of his eyes, but continued eating. Qazwini remembered how Gujastak had killed and eaten the two tomcats earlier and thought it was too late to save the cat. He saw the cat cautiously approach Gujastak's trough and extend a paw. Gujastak stopped chewing. Qazwini gasped in anticipation as the cat pulled out a piece of sinew sticking to the trough's edge, but Gujastak did not attack her and resumed chewing. The cat carried away the piece and ate it at the far end of the ledge. A little while later Qazwini saw her return to the trough, emboldened, no doubt, by her adventure. She again took away a piece from merman's food. This time she did not go quite as far to eat it as she had the first time. After she had eaten her fill, the cat leisurely cleaned herself on the ledge while Gujastak swam close by, then she jumped down and left the hall.

From that day Qazwini noticed the cat's daily appearance at Gujastak's feeding times. They shared the food and Gujastak never threatened her. Qazwini once saw Gujastak frighten away another cat who had come to quarrel with the first cat over food.

Based on empathy displayed by Gujastak and the moral principle shown in not hurting the creature that did not threaten him, Qazwini assumed the presence of intelligent choice in the merman.

Chapter 25

The copies of Abbasid court ledgers and record books sent by Tusi from Azerbaijan finally arrived. Qazwini could now corroborate and reconstruct events to learn what had motivated the court to send ibn Fadlan's embassy. Not all the ledgers from which the copies were made were in order, and some had been lost or damaged. But there was enough chronological material for Qazwini to be able to make sense of the events.

While cross-checking entries with records of the historians and chroniclers, he came upon a court document that shed more light on ibn Fadlan's mysterious mission. It left no doubt in Qazwini's mind that ibn Fadlan's embassy had been sent for the purpose of investigating the Commander of Gog and Magog.

King Almış Iltäbär's request would likely have been ignored had it not been received at the time an anonymous letter was discovered in the Wisdom Chamber and leaked to the court. Written by a high official of Caliph Wathiq's court, who had undertaken a sea journey to Volga Bulgaria decades earlier, the letter alerted the faithful that the Commander of Gog and Magog had appeared in the world. Its author claimed to have conversed with the Commander of Gog and Magog and verified that he had come on the mission to destroy the world. The official had warned that the coming destruction could yet be checked by the office of the caliph severing itself from the source of evil.

The date the letter was written, and its contents, left no doubt that its author was the mysterious green-robed emissary mentioned by ibn Fadlan. The emissary's warning, however, was unclear about the date of the promised destruction. Other than the mention of the letter in the chronicle, there was no record of it in the court register. The Abbasid travel logs from the time did not reveal such a deputation or an emissary ever being sent.

Who was the letter's mysterious author, Qazwini wondered. What was the 'source of evil', from which the letter's author warned the caliphate to detach itself, in order to forestall its destruction? Who was the individual or the group that had released the letter and to what end? Qazwini finally found a line of investigation to pursue.

Chapter 26

Qazwini considered speaking to Duraid to learn the history of the mysterious letter discovered in the Wisdom Chamber. He thought the librarian might be familiar with some lesser-known details about the circumstances of the letter's discovery in view of his family's long association with the library. Qazwini's visit to Duraid was delayed as a plague of fever broke out in Baghdad and he offered his services as a physician. When he finally called on the librarian, he learned that the old man had caught the contagion. His face looked more haggard from the illness, and his voice came in whispers. Qazwini did not bother him with his queries and left after arranging his medicine and food regimen, but he visited Duraid daily for the next few days.

On the third day, as Qazwini was leaving, Duraid propped himself up on his elbows and beckoned him to his bedside. His eyes moved wildly and his voice was agitated as he repeated to Qazwini what he had said at their earlier meeting: that the Mongols would be annihilated in the same manner as the Abbasids and the Byzantines before them.

Either the act of unburdening himself or the prospect of

the Mongols' destruction seemed to give Duraid relief; his face relaxed as he lowered himself in bed. He did not speak further. Qazwini left after Duraid had fallen asleep and he had reviewed the arrangements for his care with his attendant.

Once Duraid had recovered, Qazwini brought up the emissary's mysterious letter, but Duraid only stared impassively at him and did not respond.

Chapter 27

Qazwini continued sending regular dispatches about Gujastak to Hulagu Khan with the mail from the Baghdad court. In the latest missive to Hulagu Khan, Qazwini reported an event that he had not witnessed himself but which he believed would be of interest to anyone following news of the merman.

Qazwini arrived around noon one day for observing Gujastak's behaviour and noticed the guards huddled together, farther away from the pool than they normally stood. They spoke in low voices. The previous night, one of them had witnessed Gujastak floating in the air in the hall, and steering himself with his tail. The guard reported that Gujastak was clothed in resplendent silvery attire whose skirts extended like large feathers, and as he rose into the air he left a trail of light in his wake.

Qazwini could not reconcile the almost seraphic vision described by the guard with the sight of Gujastak loudly chewing bones in the trough during his midday meal. Shortly thereafter the merman defecated, hoisting his derriere up along the edge of the pool, his excretions coming out in a solid mass carefully passed outside the pool.

The guard's account of Gujastak's rising into the air was investigated and found unreliable since he was reported drunk on fermented milk at the time of the sighting. But it alarmed Qazwini enough to take precautions to foil any escape attempts by Gujastak. Two guards were already deputed around the pool during the daytime to ensure that the visitors did not provoke him, and to protect him against any possible attackers. Another detachment of guards now relieved them at sunset for the night shift. Even though the witness account had been dismissed as unreliable, some unknown foreboding put Qazwini on edge. He worried that the news would invariably leak, and may prompt another attack on Gujastak.

Chapter 28

Qazwini's next letter to Hulagu Khan concerned a visit Gujastak received from a troupe of slave girls, Aydan among them, and the resulting excitement. Qazwini had not included all the details of that particular event in the chronicle, however.

It was Qazwini's first encounter with Aydan after her punishment by Juvayni. The only news he had had of her since that time was that she was no longer in Juvayni's favour. Standing on the platform with the other slave girls, Aydan looked pensive.

Then Gujastak saw her and bared his fangs at her, striking the water with his tail. Aydan ignored him, but Gujastak did not let up; she absorbed his whole attention. Slowly, the gloomy air about her began to lift. She walked around the pond in a relaxed manner, looking mischievously at Gujastak. The next time Gujastak barked at her, she made fun of his form. Gujastak bared his fangs in a smile. Qazwini saw that Gujastak's presence aroused something in Aydan. Soon she was in her usual humour. In her dissolute manner she flung abuses at Gujastak, who retorted with barks accompanied by obscene gestures. Throughout this exchange, Qazwini sat at his monitoring post by the entrance, writing his observations, and quietly cursing Aydan. The sight of her feral beauty overpowered and excited him again, as it had on the fateful day he met her.

The visit came to an abrupt end. While teasing him, stroking his chin and tugging at his beard, Aydan took Gujastak unawares, and slapped him. He angrily roared and splashed water with his tail, and tried to scratch her. The slave girls rushed down the platform laughing and screaming. The guards, who had been enjoying the exchange, were drenched in water from Gujastak's splashing. They shouted at him, threatening him with lances, until he calmed down.

As the slave girls stormed out of the hall, Aydan halted for a moment to wring out the water from her sleeve. She caught sight of Qazwini, and, addressing her companions, made a comment. The slave girls looked at him, and, laughing uproariously, ran out. Qazwini did not hear what had been said. As he raised his head, he saw Gujastak leering at him. Resting his head on crossed arms over the pool's ledge, Gujastak regarded him with a smirk on his face. Qazwini wondered if Gujastak understood human speech. When Qazwini looked up again, the merman was floating on his back.

Chapter 29

A priest from Byzantine was on a visit to Baghdad. While discussing the significance of icons and images in religion with Qazwini, he gave an example from the Byzantine iconoclast dynasty that represented the Eastern Church. It provided Qazwini with a vital clue to something he had misunderstood. The priest mentioned that the iconoclast dynasty had followed the rise of Islam and believed that the glorious military triumphs of the Islamic caliphate stemmed from Islam's ban on idolatrous images. It had led it to suppress religious iconography in their dominion, too. Icon worship in the Eastern Church had revived only after the Eastern Church's defeat at Amorium.

Upon the priest mentioning Amorium, Qazwini at once recalled Duraid's words about the destruction of the Byzantines by the Abbasids. He realized that the librarian did not mean that the Abbasids had annihilated the Byzantines completely; not in the way that the Mongols had the Abbasids. He was likely alluding to the famous battle fought at Amorium over four hundred years ago, in which the Abbasids had dealt the Byzantines a humiliating defeat.

The Amorium campaign was Caliph Motasem's rejoinder to Byzantine emperor Theophilus's incursion and carnage in Sozopetra. After ravaging the habitations in Motasem's dominion, Emperor Theophilus's soldiers gouged the eyes of the male captives; they bled to death as their ears and noses were cut off. Byzantine soldiers raped more than a thousand women and dragged them away naked, as slaves, with Emperor Theophilus presiding over the atrocities. An Abbasid spy mentioned that a woman had cried out Motasem's name for help amidst the clamour.

Motasem was not quick to anger, but once ignited, his wrath was not easily put out. Sozopetra was not only his dominion, it was also his birthplace; known to him from the milk of his wet-nurses, and the childhood gardens where he had played. The caliph made a symbolic choice in selecting for his retribution the city of Amorium—Emperor Theophilus's birthplace, and Byzantium's most impregnable city—that had held in check the ambitions of great conquerors.

Everything looked inopportune for the campaign. The Abbasid astrologers had made their reckonings and announced that the stars augured the caliph's defeat. Five years into his reign Motasem still wrangled with insurrection within the caliphate's borders. His long absence was sure to allow free play for the conspirators in Baghdad. There was no certainty that he would have his authority should he return alive from the campaign.

But Motasem's mind was set. Raised a warrior, the return to campaigns and the theatre of war excited him after being cloistered in palaces, surrounded by servile, duplicitous men and their cloying chatter. The preparations for the campaign were made with a punctiliousness that matched the mission's impossibility.

Soon the day came when a poet read out the panegyric that exhorted the caliph to vengeance, and a striking force of two hundred thousand Abbasid soldiers began the march with the word 'Amorium' painted on their shields and banners. Eighty thousand servants and camp followers, and one hundred and fifty thousand pack animals followed in their train, equipped with everything, from naphtha balls for the ballistae to the herbs and clays concubines used to prettify their skin.

Motasem burnt and sacked all habitations on his way to Amorium. His general Afshin led the vanguard from another route, and the Byzantines received an early setback in a confrontation with him. Emperor Theophilus panicked, and, vacating Amorium, retreated to the Halys River's north bank.

As Motasem approached Amorium he received the first correspondence from the Byzantines. Their astrologers had concluded as well that Amorium would not be taken by the Abbasids, except at the time of the ripening of figs and grapes in winter. The Byzantines wished to open negotiations for a treaty, and reminded the caliph that should he refuse, between the many moons that lay between then and the foretold time, cold and ice would destroy his men and break his resolve.

The caliph refused negotiations, and within a fortnight attained victory, taking advantage of treachery from within the fortress city.

Amorium was a smoldering ruin by the time Motasem's retribution reached its denouement. From the burning ruins of the city a column of dark smoke rose high enough for Emperor Theophilus and his men to witness it from where they were camped. It was visible during the day from its darkness and in the night from the leaping flames rising to the skies. Theophilus was to learn of the thirty thousand slaughtered in Amorium lying exposed to carrion-eaters and wild beasts. They had found refuge neither in churches, monasteries, or houses, nor in cisterns and pits. Countless women were slaughtered in the convents and monasteries, and more than a thousand virgins given to the Mamluk soldiers and North African mercenaries to feed their animal pleasures. Another seven thousand men and women were led away as slaves. A much smaller number reached the Baghdad slave market, as more than five thousand were executed trying to escape thirst and hunger in the parched Cappadocian plains.

The Amorium campaign was a record of Motasem's victory over fate, and the terrible vengeance he had exacted. Motasem had given the lie to astrological charts. Something more powerful than planetary decrees had rewritten fate.

Chapter 30

From the profusion of records about the Byzantine defeat at Amorium, Qazwini realized that the event had been studied more closely by Christian scholars for its symbolism than other military encounters between Christianity and Islam. He did not have too much difficulty making a rough chronology of the events leading up to Caliph Motasem's capture of Amorium from the information scattered in manuscripts and chronicles, and the events that transpired thereafter. In the beginning Qazwini did not discover any mention of apocalyptic signs during the Amorium campaign. But as he read more about the conflict, details emerged which forced him to look at the whole campaign as the precursor to several disturbing conflicts that marked Abbasid history, to the day the last Abbasid caliph was trampled to death.

Upon Amorium's fall the Abbasid surveyors got busy making a detailed inventory of its inhabitants before the city's fate was decided, the spoils in gold, artefacts, and humans were apportioned, and the trek back to Baghdad announced. General Afshin brought to Caliph Motasem's notice a secretive monastery inside the fortress which enclosed a sealed dome called the House of Relics. It was said it guarded the vestiges and mementos of ancient prophets. Byzantine kings had given pledges that neither they nor anyone from their line would harm it. For centuries, in memory of that pledge, they had put locks bearing their seal on the dome's entrance.

A message was promptly sent to the custodians that the caliph wished to open the House of Relics and inspect its contents. The custodians sought a week's reprieve in order to consult with the monastery's guardians on the matter. The place was put under guard by the Abbasid commander; nobody could enter or leave without his permission.

On subsequent occasions when the caliph's officers visited the custodians to demand an answer, they were offered excuses for further deferring the matter. They spoke of the appointed hour under an auspicious planetary conjunction when the dome could be opened lest the curse of the ancients should strike them. Realizing that the custodians must not have received encouraging replies from the courts they had solicited for counsel, General Afshin pursued his case with threats of dire consequences until the custodians relented. They asked the caliph for a guarantee of their safety and amnesty from forced conversion, which was granted them.

Chapter 31

Juvayni had promised Qazwini the manuscript containing the account of the architect who had entered the House of Relics, cautioning him that it was considered by many to be a fiction. When it arrived, Qazwini was surprised at the large size and weight of the package. He saw that Juvayni had sent him, in addition to the architect's account, the philologist and zoologist Jahiz's manuscript of the bestiary *Book of Animals* in three volumes. Although Jahiz's text was the main source of Qazwini's planned cosmography, he had never seen that particular manuscript. The seals showed it was a gift sent to the Abbasid caliph Mustansir from the Mamluk dynast Shamsuddin Iltutmish of India.

The bestiary had the curious, resplendent illustrations of many creatures Qazwini had not seen in life or image before. The chapters on creatures native to India were particularly lavishly decorated. After admiring the illustrations for some time, he put the manuscript aside to peruse it at length later, and reached for the architect's report.

Architect Khalid ibn Abdullah's Account of the House of Relics

A faint buzz emanated from inside the House of Relics and slowly rose into the morning air. It articulated into distinct noises as the door's bronze bolts slid out of locks. After removing the seals and locks from the portals, the custodians anxiously stepped away, and stood behind us in a semicircle. As they chanted in undertones, we moved towards the dome, and listened through the shut portals.

It sounded as if a large beast were enclosed within. The scampering sounds and the squeak of talons on the floor accompanied powerful fluttering noises. Was some beast chasing a large bird, or a predatory bird hunting some beast? More layers of sounds were gradually added to the first ones: The rumble of thunder, the splash of water and the sweeping sound of a great wave. It felt as if the wave would crash out from the confines of the dome and sweep everything away, but the dome's portals remained closed.

The scampering and fluttering kept competing with the sound of the waves in ebb and flow until all sounds were overridden by the steadily increasing drumbeat of horses' hooves. First a few riders, then very many; thousands of troopers grew to tens of thousands; the horde increased. The custodians' chanting rose louder. The riders growled like demons, shouting and grunting malevolently. Every now and then the panicked cries and screams of women rose up amidst their uproar, and were drowned out by the demon troopers' excited barks, the drumbeat of hooves, and the violent neighing of horses. We heard the familiar grinding of rolling siege engines, the sound of Ramparts being struck with mangonels, and crashing walls burying terror-filled cries. But the demon troopers' evil presence reverberated louder still.

The sounds of scraping talons, flapping wings, and crashing waves entwined with those of the demon army, until it all became one noise. It grew fainter, and merged with the custodians' chanting, before slowly rising to a crescendo, and crashing against the dome's portals with an impact we felt between our ribs.

In the silence that ensued, the House of Relics' portals swung imperceptibly on their hinges and opened a crack. A tiny cloud of black vapour materialized between the portals that we at first mistook for dust from the lintels. It acquired a square, black form. A pair of glowing eyes that regarded us from the bounded darkness appeared within it, before the outlines spread, becoming fiery letters. The black form rose and dissolved into air.

Parting the doors, we found hanging in the air like a semi-transparent wall the faint smell of burning and dust fermented with time. We searched the dome's upper and lower levels but found nothing. Further search could not be carried out without demolishing the building. Upon emerging from the House of Relics my companions and I stopped, and looked at each other in bewilderment and disbelief. By my reckoning we had barely been inside the dome an hour or two. As I looked at the setting sun, I could not believe that we had spent half a day inside. The custodians had melted away. An armed guard was left at the dome with instructions to keep the portals open. We dispatched a report of our progress to the caliph, and awaited his orders outside the monastery. Later, we heard noises from the camp's direction, and the strange cries of a bird in the sky. Our eyes searched the sky but saw nothing.

The caliph sent four hundred auxiliaries armed with hammers, pickaxes, and a wheel-mounted battering ram, with orders to resume work without delay. By the time the sun rose over Amorium, the House of Relics had been razed, and an area marked by angular stones near the dome's rear boundary had been excavated, revealing a buried copper vault covered with iron clasps. It was brought to the caliph, and one of his bodyguards broke its seal with a few measured strokes of the chisel.

Caliph Motasem took out a reliquary of gold whose lid was emblazoned with Greek letters. A gold lock secured it, the key to which hung from it by a chain. The caliph turned the key and lifted the lid. Inside was a book each one of whose pages was inscribed with twelve lines in Greek, with accompanying symbols of men and beasts.

A group of scholars from Baghdad's Wisdom Chamber, who accompanied the caliph during his campaigns to document repositories of knowledge and decode manuscripts, translated its text into Arabic for the caliph's study, and the manuscript was entered into the Abbasid collection under Caliph Motasem's seal.

∞

The marginal note marking the text where the architect Khalid ibn Abdullah recounted hearing strange cries of the bird referred to an account of Caliph Motasem's encounter with the griffins at Amorium in the manuscript of Jahiz's bestiary. Qazwini now understood why he was sent the text of the bestiary, but it also intrigued him. He had not come upon that account in the other manuscripts of the *Book of Animals* consulted earlier.

Scholars who supervised the preparation of manuscripts of classical texts belonged to various religious schools. It happened very seldom that the author's theories were given a twist, or changed in the choice of words used. More common was the addition or removal of examples in such important works as Jahiz's text from the influence of a particular religious school or sect commissioning it. He imagined that the text was either from a particular religious school's view, or prepared by a scholar who wished to emphasize a certain event in history by highlighting the example in a classical text.

CALIPH MOTASEM'S ENCOUNTER WITH GRIFFINS AT AMORIUM

Three days before the return march from Amorium was announced, Caliph Motasem inspected the periphery of his camp and the state of the supply trains.

The sun was setting as the caliph finally turned his horse towards his pavilion. General Afshin rode a few paces behind him. Two Mamluk guards were on either side of the caliph. A contingent of trusted guards, both mounted and on foot, surreptitiously moved in a wide swathe around the caliph, to quickly close ranks in the event of danger. As the retinue passed the heart of the camp, he heard cries and the neighing of horses from the camp's western wing. A fully accoutered horse charged past him without a rider. A wave of alertness swept through the guards of his secret cordon.

The caliph reined in his horse and turned his attention to the noises. At a glance from General Afshin a soldier galloped away to make enquiries. The caliph shaded his eyes against the sun and regarded the scene from the vantage point where he had halted. He saw men running, and others crying out and gesturing, their gaze and hands pointing in one direction. Motasem could not make out the cause or source of the commotion. General Afshin shouted an alert, and all eyes followed where his hand pointed. The caliph heard the crowd's uproar, and saw one of his soldiers running towards him. The cries grew louder, as a white, leonine, eagle-headed creature charged out from behind a stone. The caliph recognized the griffin, the beast of legend known to him from the statuary, and the illuminated Byzantine manuscripts in his collection. The griffin moved too swiftly for any wild animal he knew. As it closed on the soldier, it leapt, but the soldier stumbled and fell, and the charging beast came rushing in a straight line towards the caliph's retinue.

The lancers from Motasem's outer cordon knelt on one knee, forming a row in the beast's path. The archers of the caliph's bodyguard swarmed and made a protective ring around him, arrows notched and drawn. The caliph's Mamluk guards rose in their saddles, ready to strike, holding aloft their swords with both hands. Even as Caliph Motasem balanced himself in the saddle and weighed his drawn sword in his hands, the griffin cried and leapt, its majestic head tilted, and its sides opened into huge white wings of iridescent layers.

Scores of bows twanged and arrows flew as the beast cleared the outer cordon. The caliph's mount reared, and wind from the griffin's flapping wings struck his face as it flew just above his head. It had cleared the lancers' cordon and the archers' circle in a single leap. Not one lance point had grazed it, nor an arrow touched it, as if it were made of air.

As the caliph controlled his stallion he noticed one of his Mamluk guards missing from his saddle. The griffin was now flying low over the camp, making plaintive cries, with the guard's body clutched in its fore-claws. The archers replaced their small bows with the long, heavy ones used by the rearguard. The beast flew to the camp's end where the siege engines stood, glided over the supply trains and the small lake and quicksand beyond, and turned back. General Afshin asked the caliph's permission to shoot down the griffin, but it was denied.

The griffin made another loud cry. This time it was answered from the distance. An instant later a second griffin came flapping its great wings over Amorium's walls. Dropping its prey into the quicksand, the first griffin flew towards its companion, which leapt in the air to join it. As they flew together over the Abbasid camp, headed for the distant hills, the setting star's last light caught them. The griffins shone like two coruscating suns emitting a thousand hues. They soared until they were two azure dots and finally extinguished from view.

There had been no other casualties in the turmoil occasioned by the griffins' appearance, but frightened horses had pulled down tents, and several men had been trampled on and received injuries. The bodyguard's body could not be retrieved from the quicksand, and funeral prayers were said for him by the lakeside.

The griffins' appearance caused as much excitement as fear. The caliph inspected the place in the camp where the creature was first seen, unsuccessfully searching the environs in hopes of finding its lair. Nobody had seen or heard of griffins' presence before in that region. The men wondered if the griffin first caught by Alexander in India also populated regions beyond that land. The House of Relics had been razed earlier that day, and the men asked each other if the appearance of the beasts were a result of the dome's desecration, and if more ill portents would follow in consequence.

The camp was awash in moonlight when the caliph returned. His pavilion was wrapped in layers of guards clad in mail and armed with heavy lances and bows. Torch posts manned by armed guards were set up in outreaching circles around the caliph's tent for the distance of an arrow's flight. The caliph's loyal commanders were not taking any chances. However, there was no further trouble.

As the Abbasid army began the trek back to Baghdad, some related the griffins' appearance to the discovery made at the dome inside the monastery. It was said the beasts, which represented the Byzantine Empire's emblem of the double-headed eagle, and guarded the gold treasure of Amorium,[*] had fled, completing the Abbasids' ascendance over the Byzantines.

---

[*] 'And the griffins of the Indians are, according to the tales of poets, the guardians of the gold of wisdom, sought by alchemists…'

—*Life of Apollonius of Tyana*

Chapter 32

As Qazwini reached the account's end, the oil lamp began sputtering. The moon was out and moonlight filtered through the lattice. As he got up to put oil in the lamp, he saw a flash from the corner of his eye. It was there one moment and gone the next. He stood still for a few moments wondering if it was an illusion caused by the rush of blood from getting up after sitting for an extended period. After a moment he dispelled the thought, and reflected on Juvayni's words that the veracity of architect Khalid ibn Abdullah's account was considered doubtful.

The following day when he met Juvayni, Qazwini consulted with him on his findings about the events witnessed and recorded at Amorium and asked what he made of the account of the griffins. Qazwini learned that Juvayni had not sent Jahiz's manuscript to him, nor had he seen that particular manuscript of the bestiary. Moreover, he did not recall reading any marginal note in Khalid ibn Abdullah's account. Qazwini learned by consulting the library record that an anonymous note in the catalogue linked Khalid ibn Abdullah's account to that particular manuscript of the bestiary. It could not have been added too long ago as Juvayni mentioned reading it recently. It was clearly the work of one of the scholars who had studied there in recent months but what puzzled Qazwini was how the person had linked the two manuscripts in a manner so relevant to his own research. Who could it have been, he wondered.

Chapter 33

Some slave girls in Juvayni's harem had been taken ill and he had requested a visit and diagnosis by Qazwini. A eunuch let Qazwini into the harem when he arrived, and left him there to perform his examination of the sick who had been moved to a separate room, and where, among the slave girls, Qazwini saw Aydan. He still smarted from their last encounter, but subdued his feelings as he was there as a physician.

Aydan seemed asleep. Qazwini put the essence of orange blossoms on a piece of cloth and gently daubed the beads of perspiration that had appeared on her forehead. Aydan stirred and looked at him with half-closed eyes. Qazwini could not read the expression in them. Her pale complexion had become wan. To determine her symptoms, he asked her if she had any trouble breathing, but she did not answer. Qazwini stole a furtive glance at her and saw her eyes flutter. After prescribing a potion, as he reached to take her pulse, she pulled back and, rising on her elbows, spat in his face. As Qazwini sat in shock, Aydan broke into laughter; then she rolled over from exhaustion.

Qazwini slowly rose and left her side. His feelings of

humiliation, his anger at her new affront, and any sense of power that he imagined he had over himself, were all lost when he was in her presence, he realized. He gave the prescription to the eunuch on his way out. He was glad nobody else was present in the sick room to witness the spectacle.

After his encounter with Aydan, Qazwini was not in a fit state for sober reflection. He lost two days of study.

Chapter 34

Qazwini was getting dressed for the court when the herald arrived, bearing urgent summons. He was led to Gujastak's hall where a detachment of the elite Mongol troopers stood. Governor Juvayni was talking to a heavyset man whom Qazwini recognized by the shape of his helmet even before he turned to face him. He stepped forward and made a low obeisance to Hulagu Khan.

Fascinated by Qazwini's reports of Gujastak, Hulagu Khan had arrived to view the merman himself. After giving him a brief report about the creature's doings over recent days, Qazwini accompanied Hulagu Khan to Gujastak's pool. He cautioned him that Gujastak's behaviour was erratic at best, and the Khan might not find him a perfectly compliant and tractable creature.

As Gujastak grunted and splashed about in his pool, two augurs from Hulagu Khan's entourage recited spells known to calm wild beasts. The slave girls from Juvayni's harem had also come to catch a glimpse of Hulagu Khan. Qazwini noticed that Aydan was among them. She seemed to have made a full recovery. Gujastak was surprisingly well behaved as Hulagu Khan ascended the platform's steps to inspect him. The onlookers attributed this to the Great Khan's majesty and dignity. Addressing Gujastak in Mongolian, Hulagu Khan asked if everything provided for his housing was satisfactory. Then he asked the creature a few questions about his tribe, his language, and the underwater land that was his habitat.

Gujastak made short barks, either in answer to these questions, or, as he did when excited. Hulagu Khan nodded his head with amusement. Of those present, only Qazwini felt that Gujastak understood what Hulagu Khan had said; Qazwini had caught a glimpse of comprehension in Gujastak's eyes when Hulagu Khan first addressed him.

When Hulagu Khan asked Gujastak his age, he replied by hitting his tail on the water's surface. The augurs exclaimed it signified that the years of his age were as many as the drops of water in the sea. Qazwini, listening to the augurs attentively, wondered if it was indeed possible for the duration of mortal existence to be extended indefinitely in a creature which derived its ancestry from a human and a beast.

As Hulagu Khan turned to step down from the platform, Gujastak began animatedly communicating in barks, and gesticulated by making the coupling sign with his right index finger and the left fist, to demand a female. Amused, Hulagu Khan asked if he indeed desired to mate. Gujastak leered.

Hulagu turned to Juvayni and asked what he made of Gujastak's demand. After a quick glance at Qazwini, who nodded meaningfully, Juvayni told Hulagu Khan that Qazwini would answer for him as Gujastak's keeper.

Qazwini made an obeisance and replied that pairs should ideally be found from within the species, and a merwoman would be best suited for Gujastak, but since Gujastak was half human, in his considered opinion a human female with a feral temper would also make him an excellent mate.

Hulagu Khan, who had stepped down from the platform, looked hard at Qazwini, and laughed a cruel laugh. Having sensed his commander's approval, Juvayni ordered Qazwini: 'Choose any from among the slave girls assembled here and do the will of the most exalted among men.'

A murmur of agitation and nervous laughter rose from the group of slave girls. Qazwini respectfully bowed to Juvayni, and then bowing more deeply to Hulagu Khan, stepped towards the slave girls. Gujastak barked loudly and swam in circles, as Hulagu Khan pensively regarded the scene, combing his thin beard with his fingers.

Qazwini started from one end of the group, looking fixedly at the women's physiognomy; in a couple of instances he inspected their hands to check for bulbous flesh under the nails—the sign of an unrestrained nature.

Qazwini stopped in front of Aydan, and did a perfunctory inspection of her face. She turned a poisonous look at him, and stared back impertinently. He disregarded her look, and checked her hands and thumb. The search was a pretence. When suggesting a human female to pair with Gujastak, Qazwini had already decided on Aydan on account of her unbridled, lustful nature, the fact that she had fallen in disfavour with Juvayni, and the interest Gujastak had shown in her. Qazwini was reluctant to admit to himself that his vengeful desire to punish Aydan for her insolence was a driving factor in the choice, too. Rather than acknowledge that, he told himself that if Gujastak were to mate successfully with a human female, the offspring would have the language of both parents, and could act as an interpreter between them. He could then interrogate Gujastak through the child, and learn the mysteries of the beast-humans. It was true that these advantages could not be gained by pairing Gujastak with a mermaid. From another point of view, too, Qazwini had high hopes for the experiment's success. He recalled one of Aesop's fables that answered the question whether half-beasts could successfully mate with humans: it was the story of a farmer whose flock of sheep had started giving birth to lambs with human heads because the poor shepherds, unable to afford wives, were lying with the sheep. Qazwini surmised that if humans could breed with beasts, there was an even greater chance of their breeding fruitfully with beast-humans, like the merman.

Qazwini looked at Juvayni to indicate that the inspection was complete and the choice had been made. Juvayni nodded at him with a cruel smile. Holding Aydan firmly by her upper arm, Qazwini led her out. Aydan did not try to release herself. She walked in a dignified manner, her head held high.

Gujastak had stopped barking; only a soft, continuous growl could be heard from the pool.

Qazwini noticed Aydan's breath ran a little quicker, but she did not seem perturbed or awestricken as Qazwini led her before Hulagu Khan. There was a glint of mischief in Hulagu Khan's eyes as he inspected Aydan. He asked Juvayni to find out if she was agreeable to be paired with Gujastak.

Juvayni had hardly turned his face towards Aydan to ask when she spoke, uttering each word with venomous purpose, her fierce eyes derisively regarding the three men about to decide her fate: 'His Exalted Lordship, the flower of manhood among men, should know that his slave girl would consider Gujastak a boon.'

The insolent two-edged words that questioned Juvayni's manhood incensed the governor. There was a note of triumph in Gujastak's bark when he growled and splashed, as if offering accolades. Hulagu Khan snorted and with a final look of approbation at Gujastak walked away, with Juvayni trailing behind him.

Aydan's words, and the manner of her utterance, had had a strange effect on Qazwini. The lustful, unruly creature he had selected for a vengeful experiment was transformed in his eyes by her bold defiance. To speak as she did before one of the world's most terrifying monarchs warranted a resolute courage to which only noble souls had recourse. He knew of no virtue but an animated lust that bound Aydan's soul to her unrestrained nature. But in the vessel of her body it had performed a miraculous function. Qazwini was forced to concede that Aydan's courage was bred by the fiery desire that ruled her. He believed he was wrong to hold concupiscence of little account as a mere instinct, and a device used by nature for procreation and the continuation of life.

Lust like hers was then a marvellous aspect in a human, a virtue to be valued, and a thing of wonder. Concupiscence had to be considered as a superior, multifaceted essence that shaped human character. If one took that approach, Qazwini realized, the senses that fed lust, and the resulting emotions that sustained it, must be considered sacrosanct human qualities.

He felt shame at his vindictive treatment of Aydan. The matter was now out of his hands. Hulagu Khan had sanctioned the experiment. Qazwini saw her turn to look at the slave girls, an insolent smile playing on her face. He searched in vain for any signs of despair under the mask of bravery.

Qazwini looked at the carnivorous merman and surveyed his powerful body. Gujastak had already once tried to attack Aydan. There was no knowing what might happen if he found her fully in his power. Qazwini worried for Aydan.

Chapter 35

Qazwini had his first breakthrough in his research on Amorium when he chanced upon a Byzantine monk's commentary on the Abbasid poet Abu-Tammam's renowned panegyric *The Sword is More Veracious,* composed on the event of Caliph Motasem's victory. It suggested that the bigger event at Amorium was not the defeat of the Eastern Church by the Abbasids, but the latter's acquisition of the magical *Book of Power* of the occultist and miracle-worker Apollonius of Tyana.

Protective talismans and steles constructed by Apollonius of Tyana had appeared in cities of the Eastern Roman Empire in the past. Some remembered him as a benefactor of humans who defended them against the ravages of nature with his steles and talismans—constructed from his understanding of the sympathies and antipathies between the forces of nature, the use of materials that communicated with the forces of nature, and writ in Ascharaktêres, the powerful language of deities, angels and the enlightened, to which the physical world is compelled to respond. Even the Byzantine Christian authors who condemned his talismans as the handiwork of demons, did not refute their efficacy.

A BYZANTINE MONK'S COMMENTARY ON ABU-TAMMAM'S PANEGYRIC

Abu-Tammam's panegyric spoke of the impregnable Amorium of the Byzantines as the Eternal Virgin who did not grow old even when the forelocks of Time became grey; whom even the rapacious hand of fate could not deflower; the one reckoned a prize to which even time's eternal ambition could not aspire. It spoke of the Abbasids' virile swords, which had finally churned her like a cheap harlot, the glories of whose body now feasted upon by ruin and contagion. But when Abu Tammam spoke of Amorium's heavily enchased steel gates as the virgin's symbolic maidenhead, chosen to adorn the caliph's Samarra palace, he spoke a lie. They were not the ones formerly consecrated by Apollonius as talismans, which had been melted down a year earlier, because they had become objects of superstition even for the Christians themselves. The Virgin of Amorium's maidenhead did not allude to the steel gates, but the *Book of Power* of Apollonius of Tyana preserved at an Amorium monastery for longer than a millennium, whose possession completed the Abbasid conquest.†

---

†'The Mutazilite masters at Wathiq's court later feared that Apollonius of Tyana's *Book of Power* would sooner or later destroy the Abbasids; like it did its earlier possessors, and all those who conspired to acquire it to gain or usurp power, including the caliph's nephew Abbas, and the Abbasid general Afshin.'

Chapter 36

The Byzantine monk's commentary on Abu-Tammam's panegyric was the first confirmation to Qazwini that a magical text was indeed found at Amorium. It also proved that there was logic to Duraid connecting the fate of the Byzantine Empire with the Abbasid Caliphate: the destructive element that seemed to link the three empires was Apollonius's *Book of Power*. From the Byzantines it had passed into the possession of the Abbasids.

If Duraid were to be believed, however, he had predicted a similar fate for the Mongols, which meant that the book had either passed into the possession of the Mongols upon Baghdad's fall, or was destined to.

Qazwini found it difficult to imagine that Duraid, having known the book's whereabouts, had not destroyed it or revealed its location to the world. He wondered if the *Book of Power* lay among the hundreds of thousands of manuscripts spread in different wings of the governor's palace, waiting to be discovered. Qazwini felt a thrill mixed with foreboding as he considered the possibility of the *Book of Power* unknowingly passing through his hands while he made the book selection for the Mongols at the Fall of Baghdad.

Chapter 37

The news of Gujastak's proposed mating with a slave girl had spread. An anonymous rhyme narrating the bawdy details of their nuptials circulated in the marketplace, in which Qazwini was mentioned as Gujastak's sterile wife. People discussed whether a woman should be allowed to mate with a merman.

Some days later, a rival religious scholar threw Qazwini's planned experiment in jeopardy. He gave a fatwa proclaiming that since one party was not fully human, the governor could not, under the laws of slavery, give Aydan to Gujastak.

Qazwini had not foreseen this complication. He could not recall any precedent for the legality of a match between humans and merfolk. He felt great embarrassment and consternation at his negligence, which had put Juvayni in an indefensible position. Upon further reflection, however, a solution suggested itself to him. Gujastak, as a creature invested with free will—as witnessed by him—was akin to the jinn, whose males and females had both entered into marriage contracts with humans. The historical precedent was well documented in those cases. Aydan was a heathen, and beast-humans like Gujastak could not be bound by faith, so he found a way of resolving the matter to Aydan's advantage.

Qazwini drafted a contract in which the governor manumitted Aydan and settled on her a token dowry payable in the upkeep expenses for Gujastak. In effect, the contract gave Aydan her freedom once she had mated with Gujastak. Qazwini knew of Juvayni's unforgiving nature and Aydan's grave affront. Juvayni readily agreeing to the proposal made Qazwini realize that the governor did not expect Aydan to survive the experiment.

Chapter 38

The Abbasids were the first power in a millennium to come in contact with the *Book of Power*. Like the Byzantines, who believed its possession would perpetuate their empire's power, Qazwini learned that the Abbasids, too, were informed of such glory. Through a dream in which events from private and familiar history known to Caliph Motasem were recounted to him, the *Book of Power* acknowledged the caliph as its new master, gave him encouragement, and informed him about his enemies' conspiracies. What was strange was that the *Book of Power* had taken a human form in the caliph's dream. It had appeared to Motasem in the guise of Caliph Mamun.

CALIPH MAMUN'S DREAM
ANNUNCIATION TO HIS SUCCESSOR

Caliph Motasem dreamt that he stood before a building, which he recognized from his commanders' descriptions as Amorium's House of Relics. He could feel and hear the strong wafts of wind. Scenes from his past rapidly moved before his eyes like leaves of a manuscript turning in a strong wind. A black wisp of smoke slipped towards him from between the moving scenes. It took human form as it neared, its dark cloak fluttering in the breeze. The caliph recognized his predecessor, Caliph Mamun, standing before him.

The two had participated together in several campaigns, and Mamun's eloquent speeches to troops had often moved him. Whenever Mamun called to his aid Motasem's formidably trained Mamluk battalions in time of rebellion, Motasem had never been slow to respond. Both shared a love for learning and Greek manuscripts. Motasem still carried a copy of the first Arabic translation of Ptolemy's *Almagest*, which Mamun had commissioned and presented to him.

Mamun's apparition spoke in a rasping voice, felicitating Motasem upon his conquest. Mamun recounted how he had ordered the breaching of the Great Pyramid of Cheops in a quest for the wisdom of the ancients, and advised him not to allow doubt to make a nest in his heart, now that he had secured the greatest gift.

He advised Motasem to be severe in exercising justice and reminded him that the conservancy of peace and the quelling of strife on earth was the duty of God's vicegerent. He showed him a glimpse of the horrid beasts of destruction from End Time, Gog and Magog, and told him to remain steadfast in the face of terrors, which would afflict him as the possessor of the key of power. He warned him as well to guard it resolutely from traitors whose faces he then exposed to the caliph in bloody visions.

Then Caliph Mamun fell silent and only the wafting breeze was heard. The vision disappeared as it had materialized, the body dispersing into thin, wispy black shreds, blown away into invisibility by the breeze, as the edifice of House of Relics dissolved.

—*The Book of Abbasid Dream Chronicles*

Chapter 39

While the Abbasid dream chronicler's account did not elaborate what was meant by the 'greatest gift' and the 'key of power', Qazwini surmised that it must allude to the *Book of Power*, which bestowed occult powers on its possessor. It was the first time that the full significance of the text had become known to him. The dream chronicler either did not feel the need to identify the *Book of Power* beyond an allusion to its nature, or feared taking its name.

A vision had come to alert and protect Motasem from the conspiracies being planned and the dangers that lay ahead in the guise of his predecessor's apparition. The dream had foretold subsequent events. Qazwini knew that the charge of conspiring to usurp power were later proven on one of caliph's nephews, Abbas, who had planned an ambush on Motasem on his return journey from the Amorium campaign, and he had been beheaded. Motasem's general Afshin—who first brought Motasem's attention to the House of Relics where the *Book of Power* lay hidden—had been sentenced to death later on another charge of conspiracy. Qazwini wondered if either Abbas or General Afshin conspired to kill Caliph Motasem to possess the *Book of Power*. The two men had been put to death on unrelated offences, but was there a connection between them, obfuscated by history? What could not be denied was that the *Book of Power* had already begun serving its new master since Motasem was warned about the threat in the dream.

Qazwini now felt sure that ibn Fadlan's cryptic words, too, about inscribed words and images attracting evil, could only have alluded to the *Book of Power*. If it bestowed power on its possessor, it would be desired by others seeking power; those coveting power would be stirred into taking steps to wrest it from its possessor.

The letter of the green-robed emissary had warned the caliphate to sever its relationship with the unnamed evil in order to forestall the coming destruction. It was another proof of the widely held belief about its power, and the dangers of possessing it.

There was still doubt in Qazwini's mind about the nature of the evil the letter's author spoke of. Was it a rival power faction? There were many undercurrents of intrigue and conspiracy in the Abbasid era, but anyone who would have acquired the *Book of Power* in order to possess power would have had to wield it within the Abbasid Caliphate structure. A threat to the Abbasids therefore had to be an outside force, unless ibn Fadlan's words did not directly allude to the *Book of Power*, but its nature. Those who possessed it, and ruled by its power, mentioned it with fear and reverence.

Qazwini was intrigued about the ungodly power the book's acquisition conferred on its possessor. But he wondered more about the caliph, God's vicegerent, desiring to acquire such a thing.

Chapter 40

When Qazwini investigated the events surrounding Mamun's breaching Cheops's pyramid in a quest for the wisdom of the ancients, he found the same restive, ungodly thirst for power operating there, that was a disgrace to a caliph's hallowed station.

Hints found in treatises on alchemy and astrology suggested that the sorcerer Hermes Trismegistus had built the pyramids at the time of Noah's Flood to hide pieces of his Emerald Tablet of cosmic secrets inside them. The popular belief that the Emerald Tablet was hidden underwater was a misunderstanding arising from the fact that the pyramids had been submerged during the Flood.

Caliph Mamun had commissioned Ayub ibn Maslamah, an Egyptian scholar of runes and ancient letters, to copy and translate inscriptions from the statuary, places of worship, steles, and obelisks in Egypt to learn the pyramids' secret.

Ayub was able to translate the inscriptions in Greek and Coptic, but he could not understand the hieroglyphics. In his view they were a code based on the shapes of astral bodies. The ancient Egyptian texts therefore remained inaccessible to

Mamun and strengthened his notion that a tablet that explained the code lay hidden in the pyramid. After prolonged struggle Mamun had managed to enter the Burial Chamber where he discovered human remains wrapped in strips of cotton and enclosed in sarcophagi that had been there from a very old time. The walls of the Burial Chamber were writ with the same secret notations that had evaded Mamun's efforts at translation. He called off the mission when no trace of any secret text was found inside the pyramid.

Qazwini believed that human ambition took its worst form in the quest for power. From a desire to acquire it humans recoursed to diabolical means which yoked them forever to the brotherhood of evil. Was the caliph's authority not sanctioned in the name of God, the Strongest and the Most Powerful? Why the need for profane aids in seeking or consolidating power? Did the caliph imagine that there existed a source of knowledge, such as the Emerald Tablet, that conferred absolute knowledge and power without obligation?

Chapter 41

Preparing for mating in water, Aydan trained in swimming and diving in the recently constructed pool which was twice as large as the one made for Gujastak. Qazwini improvised attire for her that covered the area from her bosom to the hips. He designed it on the principle of the horse saddle, except it was an outer shell expressing in cloth the mould of Aydan's breasts. Allowing for the limbs' unimpeded movement, it helped her to swim freely, and mate without removing the garment.

It had to be closely fitted to her body. Qazwini was obliged to take Aydan's measurements himself. The seamstress did not quite understand the ingenuity of the outfit, and how the movement of the legs opening would pull open the folds of the cloth. Much as he wished to avoid another encounter with Aydan, he discovered that the thought of once again seeing and touching her body excited him.

Qazwini looked up as the eunuch announced Aydan, and saw her approach with an impassive face. When Qazwini asked her to remove her clothes, she did so without hesitation. Qazwini picked up his measuring thread from the pedestal where his reed pen and paper lay. He turned towards her. Bathed in the light filtering from the window, her pale body looked inviting. Aydan remained still while he took the measurements, completely ignoring him, as he searched her face with sorrowful, repentant eyes as his hands moved over her flesh, touching and grazing her body. She returned his gaze with a vacant, cold look. When the measurements were finished, she left.

When the dress was done, it was sent to Aydan. When she next came for her training Qazwini saw that it fit her perfectly. She looked past him when their eyes met.

∽

Between Aydan and Gujastak there were continuous exchanges. They began with Aydan lovingly caressing Gujastak's face and combing his hair with her fingers. As Gujastak happily growled, she tugged at his hair roughly, or scratched his nose with her nails. When Gujastak howled in protest she stroked him again, cooing lovingly in his ears, but no sooner had he settled down than her tormenting him would resume. This continued until he was fully riled, at which point she withdrew to a safe distance and went away with a smirk. Gujastak barked and made profane gestures long after she had gone.

Their interactions and the ensuing uproar would greatly entertain the newly deputed captain of the guards, a stocky, broad-shouldered Tartar, who often joined Aydan in tormenting Gujastak. He had returned injured from the frontier, and was assigned to guard duty. Qazwini foresaw trouble when he saw the captain and Aydan become familiar, and wondered how Gujastak might react.

Chapter 42

Qazwini learned that Caliph Motasem's apocalyptic vision at Amorium was just the first of a series of such visions recorded during the Abbasid era. Apocalyptic phenomena became a public obsession during the reign of Motasem's successor, Caliph Wathiq. They were said to be triggered by the Syrian Christian monk Sergios-Bahira's book of prophecies, *The Apocalypse*. The monk had foretold that End Time would occur during Caliph Wathiq's reign. The widely narrated eschatological poems, the narratives of the traditionists, and the reports of transmitters were full of catastrophic tidings. Divinations by long dead saints were discovered every few days, and deranged men in the streets proclaimed themselves the Saviour. The heresies and profanations in the land multiplied daily.

Apocalyptic dreams in which people saw Gog and Magog attacking their habitations and causing destruction occurred frequently during this period. Even during the waking hours people remained under the influence of their nocturnal dreams. They felt the danger drawing closer and becoming more palpable. Convinced that the world would end, men gave up ambition. Traders stopped speculating. Slaves killed their masters to make a dash for their ancestral lands. Spouses confessed their adulteries to each other in order to lighten the burden of their sins. Everyone waited for Gog and Magog to attack after breaking free from Alexander's Rampart where the creatures had been imprisoned for ages. Awaiting the promised destruction, the economy and society came very near self-inflicted collapse, posing a danger to the caliph's authority.

Finally, the caliph himself fell victim to these dreams. His End Time dream was recorded by the Abbasid chroniclers.

∞

Caliph Wathiq's Apocalyptic Dream

Caliph Wathiq saw himself standing before a great brass wall that rose to the heavens and bound the sides of the horizon. A foetid smell floated down from beyond it, and he heard the dense tumult of a great congregation whose aggression seeped through the wall's solidity. Their ear-splitting drumming threatened to shatter the wall into pieces.

As he listened to it with growing anxiety, Wathiq saw a glow behind the metal barrier. A tongue of fire emerged through the wall and slowly spread across its surface. A dark mass eclipsed the flame, and the distant noise came near. Strange creatures approached, and Wathiq recognized his apocalyptical and supernatural enemies, Gog and Magog, as they rushed past him, their tongues hanging down from their mouths, their eyes squinting. He realized that the dark matter obscuring the flames was the creatures' escaping through the fissure in the wall. They were blinded by the world's vision that was brighter—even in the dark of night—than anything they had regarded in the miasmic darkness surrounding them since birth. The evil races, which lived in the valleys behind the Rampart, were free to serve with the forces of Dajjal the Antichrist. 'What is this wall?' someone who stood beside him asked. 'Alexander's Rampart,' he answered.

The caliph woke up as he said the words, with the smell of the flames and the horde not wholly dispersed in his memory.

—*The Book of Abbasid Dream Chronicles*

∞

Caliph Wathiq believed that the dream was prophetic. The vision of Gog and Magog's legions breaking free from the prison of iron and liquid metal was too real. Was it an omen to warn him that their hordes, said to lie dormant until Judgment Day, were about to invade his dominions?

Wathiq commissioned a map of the world which the mathematician Khwarizmi drew up with a team of seventy geographers. The exact location of Alexander's Rampart was determined and marked on the map for the first time. The Rampart's crenellated wall was shown in the extreme north-east, from which an unnamed river flowed down which meandered past the boundaries of the City of Copper and fell into the Caspian Sea.

To engage their myrmidons in the event of a breach in the Rampart, the caliph secretly dispatched a contingent of soldiers to the Abbasid borders. They would delay the enemy's arrival in Baghdad, giving the caliph enough time to gather his subjects, and surrender the souls of the faithful in an orderly fashion before God.

In the caliph's dreams the creatures' vision recurred, disconcerting him. The augurs and interpreters of dreams determined that the visions which possessed the caliph in his sleep, and overpowered his imagination during waking hours, could be counteracted with an amulet made with the names of the Seven Sleepers of Ephesus, and dust from the grotto where they slept, guarded against all terrors till the End Time. It was said that the amulet placed on the caliph's head would bring peaceful sleep to him and put him under divine protection.

Desirous of being rid of the terrible dreams, the caliph sent one of his trusted aides, the scientist and scholar Khwarizmi, on a clandestine mission to the grotto on Mount Anchilos in Byzantium.

Khwarizmi set out from Baghdad on 17 May 842. In view of the caliphate's strained relations with Byzantium, and the secrecy enveloping the mission, he could not take along a large retinue befitting a caliphal expedition. He travelled as a Christian pilgrim, accompanied by a trusted attendant. He arrived in Constantinople and presented himself in the court of the infant emperor Michael III, and solicited the regent Theodora for permission to journey to the grotto at Mount Anchilos.

Chapter 43

Qazwini tried to conjure up in his mind the image of Khwarizmi as he left for Mount Anchilos. At the time Khwarizmi was past sixty, and most of his work in mathematical explorations and geographical determinations was behind him. He had improved the geographical knowledge left behind by Ptolemy, worked out the table for the movements of the sun, the moon, and the five known planets, and furthered the research of the Indian mathematicians and the Babylonian astronomers.

Those were remarkable accomplishments, and Qazwini wondered if Khwarizmi felt a sense of restlessness as he approached life's end. Did his determinations and calculations about the universe no longer give him the sense of intellectual triumph that he once felt? Had he discovered that like the search for meaning in human existence, exactitude in sciences and mathematics was also an illusion? Did he feel, perhaps, that the inconsistent poetry of myths and legends, trivial as life itself, held greater truths? Or was it that Khwarizmi had come to understand why the Mutazilite doctrine, that put rationality at the centre of human existence, had limited influence beyond the confines of the scholars' world? That rationality was irreconcilable with human nature?

Khwarizmi returned to Samarra a month later with the dust from the grotto, which he presented to the caliph. He gave him an account of his journey and told of the strange sounds he had heard in the cave, of the drumming of horses' hooves, the cries of men, and the sounds of the engines of war. He described the cave that did not receive direct sunlight at any time of the day; yet, like precious stones carved to trap light inside them, it glowed with no visible source.

Khwarizmi reported seeing eight bodies within. Except for the body of the dog that lay beside them, seemingly untouched by the hands of time and decay, the bodies were covered in mould, plants grew out of their mouths, and their shrunken hands and feet were ossified.

Qazwini reflected on the symptoms and proposed a cure for the caliph's dream. He understood why the fear of death and losing power should manifest as apocalyptic nightmares and the sought remedy should itself be a symbol of death. The permanent somnolence of the Seven Sleepers and the dust of the grotto represented the corpse and the grave.

The weak and the vulnerable had a near superstitious faith in the protection of the caliph, the Commander of the Faithful. If the caliph himself was beset by fears, the condition passed on to those who fell under his protection. Sometimes it was a reverse process, with public obsessions guiding the caliph's imagination. Just as the caliph's mortal weakness had influenced his dreams, his superstitious belief in the cure may equally guard him and his subjects against the nightmares.

The traditional view held that the Seven Sleepers of

Ephesus were merely asleep; that they would rise on the Day of Judgement. Qazwini had read how sorcerers sometimes put themselves in a trance in which the soul could leave the body, to return years, decades, or aeons later, full of insights explored in other planes of existence. Could it be that the ossified sleepers Khwarizmi saw in the cave were alive, as the traditional view held?

Qazwini wondered if the Commander of Gog and Magog—or the Beast of the Apocalypse, as the King of Volga Bulgars described him—may also have been alive in the same way when ibn Fadlan saw his remains. Was that the reason that despite receiving the prescribed cure from Khwarizmi, Caliph Wathiq's dreams had returned, and why the plague of apocalyptic dreams had not ceased in his time?

Chapter 44

Gujastak swam with fierce strokes in the new pool to which he had been shifted. It was the first day Aydan was to share the pool with him. Along with the captain of the guards, six armed lancers stood along the pool's ledge in case she balked at entering the pool at the last moment, and had to be forced, or rescued if something went wrong and Gujastak attacked her. The guards at the pool had not been changed lest an unfamiliar face should startle Gujastak and keep him from his purpose. Aydan's female guards, too, had been similarly kept unchanged.

Hulagu Khan could not be present as he was visiting the forward positions of his troops on the eastern border, and Juvayni had refused the invitation to watch the spectacle. Qazwini felt relieved that he could pay greater attention to the experiment without worrying about protocol.

As Aydan entered the hall, Gujastak growled from the pool's far end. Qazwini checked the temperature of the pool once again. Finding it satisfactory, he took his seat in the new observation post, modelled on the lookout's post in the galleons. At his signal the seat was quickly hoisted above the platform with ropes and pulleys and locked in place.

Aydan showed no disquiet, but her female guards were anxious. Followed by them, she resolutely climbed the platform's steps.

To Qazwini's surprise, Gujastak quietly waited at the pool's far end, slowly bobbing up and down with the water's gentle swaying movement. The creature's placidity worried him. He wondered if Gujastak was biding his time before unleashing himself.

Qazwini again felt apprehensive about Aydan's safety as she stood at the platform above the pool, her dark hair newly cropped to just above her ears. Her clothing enveloped the tempting rawness of her youth. An involuntary curse escaped Qazwini's lips as Gujastak barked loudly at Aydan impudently tearing off the outfit he had made for her.

Aydan's smooth, waxen legs looked a model of anatomical balance. The upturned points of her nipples and the cleft of her sex made a propitious trine like Jupiter and Venus with the moon alongside. She looked at the Tartar captain eyeing her by the poolside and cast a fleeting glance upwards, observing Qazwini engrossed in her nakedness. The image in Qazwini's eyes of Aydan standing naked and still at the pool's edge was broken by the splash of water as she dove in.

Instead of charging towards her, Gujastak floated at the pool's other end and watched her with his jaws set, the canines showing. Aydan swam a few strokes towards him, and then waited. Holding herself upright in water, she gently moved one hand over her glistening breasts, the other placed between her legs.

Slowly, Gujastak swam towards her. Aydan still expressed

no anxiety nor made any frightened movement upon seeing him approach. The Tartar captain moved closer for a better view.

Aydan and Gujastak were now separated by a handspan but they did not yet touch. Gujastak softly growled, as he encircled her, his tail making an arc around her body. As he slid his tail between her legs, she caught it between her thighs and caressed it. Gujastak's large, rough hands clasped her body.

Aydan's slowly turned her face from the perspiring Qazwini, towards Gujastak. Then with a hiss she scratched Gujastak's face, who growled angrily, and lashed his tail across her buttocks. Aydan laughed maniacally, catching his manhood, which burgeoned like the member of Priapus at her touch. Her face flushed, Aydan leapt at Gujastak who fell on his back.

Fearing his violent retaliation, Qazwini shouted at the guards to separate them, but they stood like deaf men, watching Aydan as she grabbed Gujastak's member lurching above water, and boldly mounted him. There was a swift movement of Gujastak's tail underwater. His large hands pulled her by her hips and they coupled.

There was tumult in the water as Gujastak drove into Aydan who, moaning, sat atop him with her back arched and her body squirming over his slippery torso, like a panther trying to find a hold atop a large prey.

Qazwini felt a powerful surge of desire, when, momentarily, Aydan's face was exposed to his view. Aydan's features were distorted with a fierce beauty with her tongue pushing out of her mouth, canines gleaming against her scarlet lips. In Gujastak's forceful thrusts her eyes appeared glazed with a dark look of carnal pleasure.

Qazwini's reverie of desire was broken by a restless movement among the lancers standing at the pool's ledge. The female guards exchanged glances. The Tartar captain and a Mongol lancer nearest Qazwini's observation post moved and grabbed one of Aydan's female guards who was making small cries as she rubbed herself and tried to tear off the skirts of her robe. Another lay thrashing on the ledge, sucking her fingers, her eyes rolling wildly.

Qazwini realized it was a mistake to witness the experiment from the observation post; he should have stayed by the poolside to maintain order. He loudly ordered his seat to be lowered, but nobody answered his repeated commands. It was too risky to jump from the elevated observation post, or climb down the pole greased with fat.

He saw two lancers trying to cover a slave girl, who nimbly leapt at one while clawing the other's groin. She quickly mounted the first without letting go of the other's tool. On the pool's other side three female guards swarmed over a male lancer. Qazwini could hear his frightened and excited cries. In a far corner, another female guard tried to interrupt by main force the impending congress of two lancers in a passionate embrace.

The pool and its peripheries were covered with writhing bodies. Sounds of sighing, moaning, and crying filled Qazwini's senses and he was driven into a frenzy at the sight of the bodies rhythmically quenching their desire around him.

Gujastak let out a bark as he planted his seed in Aydan, now hoisted above his manhood. Moments later, staring into space and trembling violently, she lay atop Gujastak, caressing his huge face as he floated on his back.

Qazwini watched from his observation post, holding his unspent desire in his hand, and a loud sigh escaped his lips.

Gujastak had swum away to the pool's far end where he again lay quiet and still. Aydan sat naked, dangling her legs from the pool's ledge. She had never been affected by modesty. Qazwini reflected, with some bitterness, that if all senses associated with lust were sanctified, then shamelessness, too, was laudable, which allowed lust unrestrained play.

As he came down the platform, his eyes briefly met Aydan's. Her triumphant smile answered his angry, defeated look. He walked away, nursing a deep pain in his groin and with his mind in turmoil. He later learned that Aydan's screams and Gujastak's growls had reached the governor's palace. They made the other slave girls restive.

Once Qazwini's mind had become calm, he tried to understand what could be the meaning of Gujastak's preliminary explorations of Aydan's body, unnatural in creatures born for mating. The anticipation and enjoyment of sexual play pointed to a higher degree of intelligence.

Qazwini wished to devise some tests to ascertain Gujastak's degree of intelligence, but his focus was soon reclaimed by the events of Abbasid history as his discovery of new records identified one of its key characters, the Abbasid official Sallam Tarjuman, who wrote the account of the red-haired woman who had emerged from the gill of a giant fish, and whose name he had searched for fruitlessly in historical records.

Chapter 45

Beset by recurring dreams of Gog and Magog invading his dominions, Caliph Wathiq launched a mission to Alexander's Rampart on 30 July 842, to study any damage to its structure that might allow Gog and Magog to escape. The mission was to head north towards Caucasus, via Tiflis, which according to tradition was built by Alexander.

Wathiq considered that a publicly declared mission to ascertain an apocalyptic event might draw public focus. It could act as a stabilizing influence on the society, while serving larger political and military ends. Having himself fallen victim to the contagion of apocalyptic dreams, he had realized the power of these visions to influence people. A carefully orchestrated event controlled by him could turn away people from lesser worries.

The person chosen to lead the mission was Sallam Tarjuman, a skilled negotiator who was called a second Solomon for his command over the language of both men and beasts.

Chapter 46

Thousands of faithful stood along the path as Sallam Tarjuman and the fifty young men chosen to accompany him emerged from the Samarra palace after receiving the caliph's blessings. Men and women stretched their arms to touch them, their clothes and their mounts, so that the memory of their caresses could travel with them to the Rampart, perchance to save them from the harm and turmoil that would one day issue from it.

The young men under Sallam's command were boisterous, excited to have been chosen for the mission. Each was provided with a purse for a year's expenses, a leather-covered felt coat, and a mount with fur saddlecloth and wooden stirrups.

Sallam dutifully made his notes on the stages of the long journey to the land where the sun rose and set, marking in his map's copy the terrain where it was shown at variance in the map, and keeping a record of the expenditures. His caravan escaped a group of bandits in the Spring of the Sands. In the Fount of Bitter Water they lost men to a mysterious disease that turned saliva into blood. They continued to press onwards and arrived in the habitation called the Shameful City of Camul whose women offered their bodies to the visitors in return for any tales they might tell them from their lands and journeys. They would later embroider and narrate these stories to their men. Sallam's men told the women about the lake where spectres of men cheated death by making barters with the devil, and were seen by sailors walking over water and sometimes heard addressing them in Greek.

The painted faces of Camul's gods leered at Sallam and his men from the wooden houses' ceilings as they satisfied their desire. In the morning when they rose, their minds were full of the legends of Gog and Magog, which the women had wordlessly transferred to them in their sleep.

For months afterwards, Sallam's party journeyed like men possessed and suffered heavy losses in lives before they reached a land where a dark sun rose, the air was foetid, and the land stretched in an interminable carpet of black soil. Along it were the beacon towers to be lit when Gog and Magog were released. They passed the countries earlier ravaged by Gog and Magog when they were at large. Scenes of death and destruction paraded before their eyes for seven days. They covered their mouths and noses with the folds of their headgear steeped in vinegar to fortify themselves against the perverse smell of half-alive corpses which inhabited the place.

On the way to the Rampart, Sallam and his men passed piles of huge brass cauldrons and ladles, in which metal for constructing the Rampart was melted. They saw the wall's leftover iron bricks stuck together with rust. There was the moat in which the Rampart gates had been cast, where the copper was melted, and the lead and copper blended by the ageless tribe of the jinn who had taught alloy-making secrets to Solomon.

They came to a mountain gorge and saw the pass from which Gog and Magog would fan out over the world's surface. Upon entering the gorge, Sallam and his men encountered the smell of carrion and heard loud whispers in an unknown language uttered by the spirits that dwelt within.

They finally arrived at the Rampart, a mass of metal and bolting mechanisms, guarded by a line of soldiers. A hundred pillars cast from meteorite iron supported the Rampart's foundations whose top was obscured by the clouds. It was constructed with alternating horizontal copper and iron bars, and had a thickness of five cubits. Sallam saw the following words written on its portals: *The Promise that is made shall be kept and this gate levelled by the hands whose work is not immediately manifest.*

Sallam asked the soldiers if they had seen any people from the races of Gog and Magog. He was told that a group was once seen above the mountain behind the Rampart. They were about four or five spans long, and looked like little Abyssinians. A powerful black gale had swept them away, either back into their land or the sea beyond. Stories were heard of sailors encountering them in turbulent waters, but the reports were dismissed as manic visions of seamen in distress. The soldiers assured Sallam that for all they knew, the evil races were secure behind the Rampart.

Sallam later inspected the Rampart's wall and discovered a hairline crack in its gate. He inserted his knife and scraped bits of rusting metal from the crack for presentation to the caliph as a memento from the Rampart.

When Sallam arrived in Baghdad twenty-eight months

later, the arduous journey and sickness had taken its toll on his troops. Of the fifty men who had set out with Sallam, only fourteen had returned.

Sallam gave Caliph Wathiq an account of his journey, reassuring him that Gog and Magog were secure behind the Rampart, and presented the iron filings from the Rampart as proof of his journey. The caliph offered praise to God, ordered Sallam's statement to be recorded and sealed. The iron filings were preserved as a relic.

Chapter 47

As Qazwini searched more thoroughly for accounts and sources for details of Sallam and his mission, he discovered that Sallam's seal appeared on important official correspondence from the eras of caliphs Motasem and Wathiq. But his mission had gone unmentioned in two of the period's most authentic records, Dinawari's *Book of General History* and Yaqubi's *Chronicle*. The latter even mentioned Alexander's Rampart but remained silent about Sallam's mission. A man of Sallam Tarjuman's stature who led a caliphal mission at a turbulent period had disappeared from Abbasid records as if he never existed.

Delving deeper into the period documents, Qazwini made the discovery that another version of Sallam's account existed in which he journeyed by sea, although it was only mentioned by some lesser-known historians, and there was a suggestion that Sallam's sea journey was a fiction that grew from a letter whose details were narrated by the storytellers of Baghdad.

According to this other version, instead of the northern direction recorded in the other versions, Sallam undertook the journey in a galleon in a northwesterly direction, where

Volga Bulgaria lay. Ibn Fadlan's account also described the caliph's green-robed emissary visiting Volga Bulgaria by sea. Was Sallam's sea journey a detour undertaken on his mission, or a separate, later mission kept secret by his masters? It seemed unlikely to Qazwini that Sallam would have commissioned a galleon and visited Volga Bulgaria on his own initiative.

Chapter 48

The plague of apocalyptic dreams begun in the time of Caliph Motasem did not end with his immediate successor Caliph Wathiq either, Qazwini had discovered. It resurfaced, eight decades later, in the time of Caliph Muqtadir.

Such dreams had not occurred during the preceding Umayyad dynasty, or even during the reign of the early Abbasid caliphs. First experienced by Caliph Motasem at Amorium, they had begun with the Abbasids coming into possession of the *Book of Power*.

The visions appeared to the *Book of Power*'s possessor, Qazwini realized, as foretold by Caliph Mamun's apparition in the dream. Driven by fear, on the caliph's part, or his court's, they compelled them to investigate if the danger they sensed was real, and if the End Time had finally arrived. Fear was a door the key of power invariably unlocked.

A theory as to why ibn Fadlan's embassy was sent to Volga Bulgaria was beginning to formulate in Qazwini's mind: the anonymous letter may have been a catalyst, but the embassy to Volga Bulgaria was prompted by the apocalyptic dreams seen by Caliph Muqtadir and members of his court, and the threat felt by them.

Qazwini's researches had brought him back to the events where he had begun them, and to the mysterious green-robed character who spoke to a beast.

To Qazwini, the identity of who released the letter warning about the commander of Gog and Magog was no longer important. It did not have to be someone adversarial to Caliph Muqtadir who hoped to create strife and weaken the caliph's authority by releasing the letter; it could equally be someone trying to strengthen the caliph's hand by raising the spectre of an external threat by making the letter public.

Determining the identity of the letter writer, on the other hand, offered clues to many mysteries. All the evidence seen by Qazwini in his research pointed at Sallam Tarjuman as the letter's author and the mysterious green-robed emissary.

Qazwini could not understand how the events unfolded following Sallam's return. Two important questions were unanswered: Why was the Abbasid high official Sallam sidelined upon his return from a successful mission that had the full support of the caliph and his court? And, what made Sallam break from Caliph Wathiq's court and take matters into his own hands?

Qazwini had to conclude that the trouble could only have arisen during or after Sallam's last recorded audience with the caliph.

Qazwini tried to read what he could find from the period when Sallam arrived from his mission. One of the first events he came upon for the period was the capture and beheading of the heretic Khadish. He also learned that a year before Sallam's return the economy had picked up as new trade routes opened. At the time of Sallam's return, the caliphate was stable, and commerce thriving. Upon entering Baghdad, Sallam must have seen the marketplaces full and bustling with activity. Many fortunes had been made in his absence. Apocalyptic narratives never flourished in times of prosperity. With the revived economy, the eschatological prophecies had died out. There must have been only a cursory interest in the details of his journey. Many would have forgotten about his mission. Caliph Wathiq was busy supervising the development of the imperial Abbasid city of Samarra that was fast becoming a rival to Baghdad in its glory with heavy investment of the state revenues.

Had Sallam learned of the *Book of Power*'s connection to the perils it invited? Was it during his audience with the caliph that Sallam explained to him the connection between Gog and Magog and the *Book of Power*? The caliph and his court not trusting Sallam's testimony was improbable, considering that—as evidenced by ibn Fadlan's embassy—the Abbasids had remained engaged with the idea of the Commander of Gog and Magog since Sallam's mission.

Could it be that Sallam's requests were not heeded because Sallam spoke of destroying the *Book of Power*, a prospect not acceptable to the caliph and his court? Another possibility could be that Sallam may have evolved an entirely different view of the *Book of Power* after his perilous mission, and come to consider it as a profane aid to consolidate power flowing from divine authority.

In either case, Qazwini could see how the demand of destroying the *Book of Power* would have sounded as a threat to anyone wielding power. Did words spoken by Sallam during his meeting with the caliph seal his fate?

In his letter to the Abbasid subjects, the green-robed emissary had clearly hinted that the *Book of Power* should be destroyed. He had demanded that the rulers dispossess and divest themselves of a power that threatened the safety of their subjects. It was a call for the purification of the centre of power. That there must have been a growing audience for those who believed in impious forces coalescing around the caliphate was implicit in the execution of Khadish. Sallam's report of the Commander of Gog and Magog would have lent weight to Khadish's claim and made him a martyr to a greater number of people. Sallam must have been considered a threat by the court.

Qazwini realized that if the Abbasids had imposed silence upon Sallam, he might have considered it his duty to God to inform the faithful, despite obstructions by the court. Did a thwarted Sallam release the letter as a test to find out if he enjoyed any support among the high officials? It was unlikely that Sallam did not have powerful supporters in the court before he left. But power interests kept constantly realigning themselves, and while Sallam may have had access to them, and, perhaps, even had their sympathies, they may have disagreed with him on the wisdom of making the letter public. The proof was that the letter was suppressed, until its reappearance a half century later during Caliph Muqtadir's reign. Something may have changed in the fifty years in the interests of powerful courtiers and their successors, making it opportune then to release Sallam's letter which had not been forgotten by them.

But it was also unlikely that Sallam's friends in power would have completely abandoned him in his time. If they thought that Sallam had offended the caliph, they may have asked him to keep away from both Baghdad and Samarra for a while. His presence in the city and absence from the court on account of the caliph's coldness towards him would have given rise to gossip that would have been dangerous to Sallam's safety, and, by association, to their own.

Could it be that Sallam's friends suggested he undertake a second mission to Volga Bulgaria from where the intelligence of the Commander of Gog and Magog had probably already arrived? Did someone suggest that he gather further evidence of the threat by documenting the events in Volga Bulgaria? It would have made sense for Sallam's supporters to keep him and themselves out of harm's way by that ruse. Apparently, Sallam followed the advice. But what course did he take upon his return to Baghdad from his mission to Volga Bulgaria when he still felt the same sense of powerlessness and continuing disregard from the caliph?

Qazwini knew that authors of apocalyptic writings were often those who had lost power and hope, or men who served God faithfully amidst people hostile to them. They spoke the truth as they saw it. Sometimes, when God's messengers had fallen silent, they spoke in their stead.

Qazwini imagined a raddled, careworn Sallam, taking his message directly to the faithful, by addressing himself to people in the marketplace, and narrating what he had seen of the Commander of Gog and Magog. He would have been one among the many storytellers who spoke of outlandish creatures, the beast-humans and such. It struck Qazwini that Sallam might not have looked too different from the old librarian Duraid, who warned people and invoked terrors in the marketplace.

Sallam's narrative could have been ridiculed by the caliph's spies who, no doubt, kept an eye on him. His story may have been dismissed by his listeners as a fabrication. The authorities would not have felt any further need to silence him, but it was clear that they had suppressed court records, and occluded history written later, to erase the memory of his existence.

Chapter 49

An alkaline smell rose from Gujastak's pool and hung about the hall. It floated into the neighbourhood around sunset and grew stronger over days. It was noticed that it brought on overpowering, maddening desire. Men hurried home and rushed into coition even before they had washed the grime off their feet. If the door to a house were left open, strangers were often found having congress, or lying naked in each other's embrace. Some thought the world might be returning to an older, happier order, as it was seven centuries earlier in the age of jahiliyya, the golden age of paganism, licentiousness and great poetry.

At the governor's palace the powerful smell invaded Qazwini's nostrils every evening when he retired to his chamber to write. His work on the cosmography had not progressed. His mind and senses were occupied with Aydan, who seemed more distant than ever.

Qazwini rose from the carpet, and stepped to the window where the waxing moon's outline, visible since the sunset, had become sharper. A slave girl lay beside the scattered folios of a work he had consulted earlier in the evening. He was replete with the aftertaste of pleasure. The release of desire had emptied his mind of all thoughts. Upon hearing the rustling sound behind him, he dismissed the slave girl with a gesture of his hand.

When he considered the chaos and violence that was so much a part of human life, and to which he must submit as the workings of fate, he reconsidered the value of scholarship, something he had long thought the pinnacle of human existence. Often nowadays, when he sat down to write he questioned the purpose of his efforts and wondered about the futility of the exercise. What was human effort worth if existence itself were so worthless and prone to be stamped out with terror? Why not scatter it away in pleasure-seeking and devote himself to tending to his lust?

Yet, he could not quite rid himself of the feeling that dull and futile as all literary and artistic endeavours seemed before the pleasures of the flesh and the apparent purposelessness of life, they were yet the only contrivance that offered those like him a defence against gratuitous indolence and reckless abandon.

Chapter 50

Qazwini was surprised to receive a visit from Duraid. He appeared to have been restored to health, although he remained frail and his eyesight had worsened. Duraid requested his help in getting work as a cataloguer at the library. The old man had spent his entire life amidst books. In his last days he wished to find in them again some purpose for his life. Qazwini wrote a note for the cataloguing department as requested by the librarian, where the old man thought he might help despite his failing eyesight. Qazwini did not think it proper to press him further about the *Book of Power* and the events at Amorium.

Qazwini had been unable to find traces of the *Book of Power* in historical references beyond the tenth century. Since the *Book of Power*'s discovery at Amorium, the Abbasid occult collection had continued to grow, and the Mutazilite scholars at the court had encouraged their study. But from the tenth century when Caliph Qadir assumed power, and helped the religious scholars gain ascendency over the Mutazilite philosophers, all mention of it disappeared from the books.

The Mutazilite doctrine of determinism had served its

political purpose for the Abbasids against the Umayyad dynasty. It had made the worldly order and the state sacrosanct, and by association the caliph's office, too, was made immune to criticism. With the Abbasids' political power fully coalesced in the institution of caliphate, it was time to suppress the doctrine in anticipation of future political and ideological challenges.

The later Abbasids set about methodically destroying Mutazilism's intellectual heritage to poison the wellspring. The teaching of philosophy was banned from the madrasa curriculum. The occult texts, too, were suppressed as part of the effort to curtail the freedom of knowledge acquisition, and their copies were confiscated and burnt. The weak and superstitious Caliph Qadir was too afraid, however, to completely destroy the occult texts, lest their annihilation invite a curse on him, or he fall victim to some magic for which a counter-spell could only be found in the collection itself, so a copy of each text was preserved in a secret underground crypt.

The memory of the crypt and its proscribed texts was not forgotten. Qazwini had learned of many efforts to locate and access the texts in the years since they had been hidden away in the crypt, and read about attempts that were foiled to break into it.

Almost a century before Baghdad's fall, the floor sank in one of the Wisdom Chamber halls. The librarian who investigated the cause discovered the entrance to the crypt and learned that through the fissures developed over time in its sealed walls, insects and dust had broken through and got to the manuscripts kept there. Qazwini could not imagine that the *Book of Power* was not among those texts. It would have been destroyed had it been kept in the crypt. There was no reason to believe otherwise as the Abbasids' political and military influence had steadily declined over the centuries. Qazwini realized that if Duraid believed that the Mongols had inherited the *Book of Power* from the Abbasids, he must have meant it as an abstraction, the Mongols being the ruling power.

Chapter 51

On a day when Gujastak's pool was scheduled to be cleaned and refilled, and Qazwini had taken a break from his observation duties, Aydan injured her head. She maintained silence about the injury and refused to answer Qazwini's queries. He inspected Gujastak's body closely for any signs of injury, suspecting an altercation between the two, but found none. He could not ascertain the facts as no witnesses were found. Later he learned that on the same day that Aydan had been injured, the captain of the guards had also broken his shoulder by slipping and falling down from the high platform. Aydan's injuries quickly healed and in the coming weeks Qazwini forgot about the incident in the excitement of the discovery that she was with child.

Chapter 52

Duraid had proved useful since resuming his labours at the library, Qazwini had heard, although he had not met him since, as the librarian came and went at odd hours. Qazwini was determined to resume work on his cosmography, and wished to see Duraid, whose memory of old manuscripts could serve him well in his research. He also hoped to renew their acquaintance, as their previous encounters had taken place under strained circumstances. One day, while passing by the neighbourhood where Duraid lived, Qazwini thought of calling on him.

He was about to knock at the librarian's door when he heard the sound of sobs and lamentations. He recognized Duraid's voice mourning his lost son, and invoking destruction on the Mongols. Qazwini turned away in sadness. He had no children of his own, but he could imagine how the tragic loss of a grown-up son could devastate a father. Despite the carnage inflicted by the Mongols on Baghdad, and on his hometown, Wasit, Qazwini did not wish for their destruction. The Mongols were doing what every empire before them had done: destroying the nurseries of culture and learning founded by their predecessors before setting up their own. The lion in the desert sought out and killed every offspring of the old lion and lioness, before coupling with the same lioness to beget cubs of his own. It was a terrible principle with power to take pride in that alone which it had created.

Chapter 53

After the passing of a lunar year, a male child was born to Aydan and Gujastak. Qazwini had closely monitored the couple's conjugal life and attended the childbirth. The child did not have Gujastak's webbed hands or tail, but he had inherited his father's fangs.

Qazwini's plans of deciphering Gujastak's language and discovering the secrets of the seas were foiled because Aydan rapidly began losing her language after giving birth. Her speech, too, slowly began resembling Gujastak's. It seemed that she had begun to consider herself a creature of water, a half-beast. Noticing her transformation, which he recognized was not a pretence, Qazwini ordered the couple to be separated. Both Aydan and Gujastak fought furiously when the guards tried to remove Aydan from the poolside. Thereafter, Gujastak attached himself to her body whenever someone came nearby. Their skins fused; short of cutting them apart, it was impossible to separate one from the other. Qazwini finally gave up, ordering that the pair was not to be separated. He could not explain Aydan turning into a mermaid from the history of beast-humans nor was there any precedent among the human species for the change she underwent.

The child kept close to his parents. He had the laugh of a human baby but spoke in the same barks and growls as Gujastak. While the child never uttered a word of the human languages he was exposed to, Qazwini believed that he likely understood both Arabic and Mongolian to which he was daily exposed, and that through him Gujastak learned more of the human language than he had until then.

Qazwini observed Gujastak playing with his son as would a human, carrying the child on his shoulders as he swam. They splashed about in water; the child slid down his lower body and swam about catching his tail. The child's laughter and Gujastak's growls echoed in the hall.

Qazwini noticed at the same time Aydan and Gujastak becoming aloof. The Tartar captain was often seen in the hall, and Qazwini sometimes caught him exchanging glances and words with Aydan. When he noticed Aydan looking at the captain with longing, something again stirred in Qazwini's heart. He wondered if Aydan was attracted to the Tartar captain, and felt jealousy fill his heart. It was strange that he had felt no such emotion at Aydan's relationship with Gujastak. Aydan's interaction with the captain only elicited a few displeased growls from Gujastak, but he did not show any hostility and kept away from Aydan's side of the pool.

Despite her withdrawal from Gujastak, Aydan remained deeply attached to her child. One day, Qazwini overheard her singing a lullaby that spoke of the child becoming a great amphibian hero.

Qazwini wondered what would happen to Aydan when the Tartar captain left. The Mongols were in the midst of another campaign. Qazwini had heard of Hulagu Khan's urgent call for troops for the impending battle against the Mamluks. The Mongol forces in Baghdad were thinly stretched. Juvayni had informed Qazwini that the guards protecting Gujastak would be dispatched with the reinforcements. For the present, he would send replacements from among his harem guards.

Chapter 54

Qazwini finished work at a late hour. He had resumed work on his cosmography after a period of time. Stepping out of the reading hall one night, he stopped as he caught a glimpse of something shimmering in the hallway. He realized that neither Juvayni nor the library clerks could be there at that hour. Noiselessly stepping forward, he reached the tower of newly bound manuscripts where he had seen the bright flash. Even though he found nobody there, the sense that he was not alone in the place did not leave him.

As Qazwini waited, he heard a faint, but steadily rising, droning noise. It sounded like a lamentation: a slow, painful yet subdued scream uttered in a language he could not understand. As he looked around to locate its source, a creature covered in glowing raiment floated into his view, gliding between the towers of books at the far end of the hallway. The skirts of his glittering robe reached down, extending like a bouquet of large feathers, just as the drunken guard deputed at Gujastak's pool had described. The droning sound came from the creature. Listening to it carefully, Qazwini realized they were spoken words, words of an incomprehensible language recited at a speed impossible for a human being, but which seemed remarkably and distinctly articulated even though he could not understand them.

Qazwini was overcome by a powerful sense of awe such as he had never felt even in the caliph's or Hulagu Khan's presence. It was a feeling of being in a majestic presence, both timeless and immortal. Qazwini then saw someone rushing out from behind a corner with a raised arm and striking the creature. With a cry the creature turned around. Even in the transformed features that glowed like amber, Qazwini recognized Gujastak's thickly veined face; his blazing fangs flashed in a mouth open with fury. The next instant the creature struck the attacker and Qazwini heard a cry as Gujastak rushed past him into the vestibule. The impact hurled Qazwini across and he hit a wall. He saw Gujastak fly out of the hall with a wailing sound and disappear, leaving him in darkness that slowly closed on his senses.

When Qazwini came to it was close to dawn and he was alone in the library. At a little distance from him he found Duraid lying in a pool of blood, his one outstretched hand holding a manuscript, the other closed around a dagger's hilt. Duraid's body was already cold. Inspecting the neck wound Qazwini saw that an animal bite had severed the jugular.

Qazwini picked up the manuscript that lay beside the dead man and opened it. Written on skin, it had the seals of all Abbasid caliphs from Motasem up to Qadir in whose reign it was buried in the crypt with other occult texts. The *Book of Power*, the Abbasid occult collection's most important text, had survived. Under the talismanic seal of Kabikij, the Lord of Insects, it had remained untouched by weevils, termites and silverfish. The Angel Raphael's name emblazoned on the binding had protected it from the elements.

Chapter 55

Qazwini wondered how the *Book of Power* had been passed on to Duraid. It was possible that the library official who discovered the crypt was one of Duraid's elders. He guessed that it was already in the library, hidden among the books the librarian had selected to remove from the Wisdom Chamber on the fateful day his son was killed. It was also possible that Duraid had lost the *Book of Power* after the Fall of Baghdad. At the time he had discovered the mysterious cross-referenced entry between the architect Khalid ibn Abdullah's account and Jahiz's bestiary, it had seemed too far-fetched to imagine that someone else was also trying to connect the dots, and assembling together the missing facts of the events he was researching. It was unlikely that Duraid had come upon the *Book of Power* at that hour by chance. Clearly, he was secretly researching the same events in an effort to locate the *Book of Power* and had found it.

Qazwini wondered why Gujastak had attacked Duraid. Just as there was no rationale for Gujastak to be in the reading hall, there was no reason for Duraid to be armed with a dagger. Why had the old librarian feared that someone might attack him? Was there a connection between Duraid and Gujastak, or between Gujastak and the *Book of Power*? Similarly, Qazwini could think of no explanation for the remarkable transformation he had witnessed in Gujastak, which corresponded exactly with the earlier recorded account of the Mongol guard about a shiny creature floating in the hall. From what he had seen, Gujastak was not a beast-human but a beast-seraph, although he could find no possible way to explain such a creature, or fashion a theory of existence to rationalize it.

Qazwini learned later that Gujastak and his family had disappeared sometime in the night. The harem guards on duty in the hall had been drugged. Qazwini concluded that Aydan had arranged it through her connections in the palace kitchen. His request for a search party to be sent for Gujastak was not granted by Juvayni, who seemed only too glad to be rid of Gujastak and Aydan, although he told Qazwini that the Mongol forces were already too burdened to be sent in search of them, and reminded Qazwini that he himself no longer had any claim on Aydan, having manumitted her at Qazwini's suggestion.

Juvayni had informed Qazwini of his worry that the campaign against the Mamluks might get prolonged. As the governor of Baghdad he was required to attend to the dispatches from commanders, provide counsel, and help set up supply routes. Qazwini saw that the thought of the impediments daily growing to his own work made Juvayni wretched. He decided not to persist with his request.

Chapter 56

Qazwini continued his investigations into the disappearance of Gujastak and his family. While interrogating a slave girl in the governor's harem, he solved an earlier mystery. When pressed to recall anything unusual she might have witnessed at any time prior to Aydan's disappearance, the slave girl remembered a water-carrier lingering outside the hall on the day Aydan was seen with the mysterious injury to her head. Later, the slave girl had seen the same person peeping through a hole in the wall. The water-carrier was found and interrogated. He was among those who had cleaned and refilled Gujastak's pool that afternoon. Assured by Qazwini that no harm would come to him if he told the truth, he confessed to spying on Gujastak through the hole in the wall. Having heard many rumours about Aydan and Gujastak's lecheries, he had stayed behind to catch a glimpse of them together.

He told Qazwini that on that day the captain of the guards had released the morning shift earlier than usual. The pool was cleaned and refilled, but Gujastak had not been moved back from the smaller pool in the adjoining hall where he was shifted during the cleaning. The Tartar captain told the men that the guards of the evening shift could move Gujastak back into the pool. Female guards were no longer deputed for Aydan by that time. She used as living quarters a tent equipped with basic necessities set up for her in a corner of the hall.

When Aydan returned to the hall from seeing her son playing with Gujastak in his pool, she found herself alone with the Tartar captain. She went inside her tent to wait for Gujastak. The water-carrier heard the captain call out to her. When Aydan did not respond, he approached her and tried to pull her towards him. Aydan fought back, and he hit her head against the ground. She managed to shout for help but the hall was deserted. As the captain tried to have his way with her, a growl echoed in the hall. According to the water-carrier, Gujastak had appeared suddenly behind the captain. The next moment the captain was flung out of the tent. He struck the pool's wall, and lost consciousness. The water-carrier had run off, afraid that Gujastak would attack him too if he were caught watching.

Chapter 57

More clues to Gujastak and his family's disappearance were found when the Tartar captain's decomposed body was recovered from behind a dune outside Baghdad. The nature of marks on his neck was the same as had been found on Duraid's. A sharp-toothed animal had chewed through his neck. Qazwini wondered if Aydan had promised herself to the Tartar captain in return for his help in smuggling herself and her child out. The earlier altercation between Aydan and the Tartar may have happened as he tried to secure his reward. It finally made sense why Gujastak had not grievously harmed the captain of the guard upon his molesting Aydan, and why she had not complained. But with her and their child safely out, Gujastak must have turned on the Tartar to settle the score. Qazwini could not ascertain the extent of the guards' involvement in their escape from interrogating them as he had hoped. Meanwhile, all men sent for the campaign against the Mamluks were killed in the battle of Ain Jalut.

Qazwini spent days searching for Gujastak's family in the desert but found no trace of them. The governor's spies had been ordered to keep an eye on any unusual cargo movements.

A spy at the Basra port reported that some days ago a large wooden box had arrived with a caravan from Baghdad and was loaded on to a Byzantine galley. It could not be searched by the port officials, as it displayed the Baghdad governor's seal. There had been some panic among the labourers who carried it aboard when it was being loaded, and later a search was ordered for the person or persons who accompanied it, but the woman with her strange looking child, who had accompanied the box had disappeared. The galley left without the pair, the wooden box aboard.

The spy kept sending Qazwini reports of a woman and a ghoulish child seen wandering the port at night. They shied away from anyone approaching them. Qazwini wondered if Gujastak, separated from Aydan and their child, might return in search of them.

Chapter 58

Qazwini had withheld the *Book of Power*'s discovery from Juvayni, realizing that as a senior functionary, he could be tempted to keep the book in the Ilkhanid Mongol dynasty's possession to serve its empire. Qazwini could not decide on the wisdom of sharing his discovery without first studying the *Book of Power*'s contents.

He carefully turned the folios of the *Book of Power* that began, like all grimoires, by placing the reader under a compact to the occult forces commanded by the book:

∽

The Compact

The author, Apollonius of Tyana, says that you are fortunate and blessed and the master of a rare gift if you find this book in your possession, for the world is in favour; of a certain your desires and ambitions will come to fruition, and from it you shall receive much advantage. My glory and honour, my consummate virtues and excellent talents, my exalted gifts and the illustrious rank where I sat draped in accomplishments were on account of this wisdom, transferred to me one day in the future and the past when the sky and the planets were or will have been in an auspicious conjunction. It was concealed in the reliquary when Virgo was ascendant as Mercury was in Virgo; the moon was in Gemini under Mercury's rule; and Saturn was in Capricorn. This wisdom shall be protected until such time that another lover of occult knowledge should find it.

Upon acquiring this book, which confers power on the one who possesses it, you must offer gratitude to the Creator, and take all measures to guard it from the world's eyes, so that it does not fall into the hands of the uninitiated, lest they should use it to profit from malevolent deeds. There are few who are deserving of its wisdom, and countless who seek it.

With the possession of this book, which is a powerful talisman, you have inherited a pledge to fulfill the compact set for its possessor. You commit to a promise and an obligation to the dead to keep its contents secret so that they are not revealed or communicated in any wise to another, for its sharing would cause derangement in the order of things and powerful tumults and disturbances to follow.

—*Book of Power*

∞

The seals of several Abbasid caliphs under the compact indicated their obedience to it. A record of past and foretold events followed, with a description of talismans that could forestall or reverse them. The *Book of Power* was, however, unique in its construction in that its author, Apollonius of Tyana, whose account was given at the end, had described the entire text as a talisman. He gave the story of a sorcerer and a mermaid whose fates were rewritten by him into a talisman, and bound in its text.

THE TALISMAN

I, Apollonius of Tyana, am the one whose memory was enshrined in parallel and contrary legends. In the first of the two histories told of my existence, I was a devotee of wisdom who served its cause no matter where it took me, from the temple of Aesculapius at Aegæ, where I learned the annunciations, interpretations, and the rationale of dreams for the purposes of healing; to the land of the yogis who lived under the sun and the moon without breathing, drinking, or eating, and who taught me to ascend the nine heavens by the celestial virtues of self-abnegation, submission, and servitude to God. I was the one who spoke the language of men as fluently as I did the speech of birds and beasts; a benefactor of humans who defended them against the ravages of nature with my steles and talismans which checked the fury of the sea stirred by the monster tanneen, the power of the wind released from the nostrils of the custodian of storms where it was kept chained, and the charge of vermin and predators when bidden by the forces of the Adversary. I was the one who, like Janus, could know the past and the future from the power of my daemonial nature; the one possessed with the ultimate gift—the power to resurrect the dead.

In the other history known of my existence, I was a sorcerer whose career grew like a vine upon the destructive plant that brought naught but remorse. I was the one who committed to the service of magic and goetia no matter where it led me—from the temple of Aesculapius at Aegæ, where I learned how to send dreams of furious visions into the minds of men to destroy their resolves; to the land of the yogis who worshipped Satan and his many faces, and with whom I rode the griffins and the manticores to climb to the heavens at night and listen to the whisperings of the angels in which they initiated me. I was the one whose abominable talismans summoned demons with the promise of unholy sacrifices, and marked with damnation all those who benefited from them. I was the one who interfered with divine work by creating discord and interruptions in the cosmic flow from the power of goetia, and facilitated the Adversary and his agents; the one who, upon the breaking of the celestial clockwork, would rise from the shell of the earth astride the Beast of Destruction to kill the pulse of life.

These diverse histories are neither true to, nor contradict my memory, but they would remain impermanent and inconclusive for I had exceeded the bounds of Time, and the circulations of my breath have not yet ceased. Until the universe is enclosed by a time where Past, Present and the Future stand still, I, Apollonius of Tyana, shall live, and my word will hold. For mine is the dominion over the elements as well as over Time; I have the greatest power over words with which I can reordain fates by weaving them into talismans.

Know then, that this talisman which also records the history of its construction, binds not only the fates of those mentioned, but also those who come into contact with the events it narrates. It affects those who were alive when what is told here came about, and also those who had shall live while the talisman exists.

∽

King Alexander of Macedon conquered both corns of the world, from the east where the sun rose, to the west where it set, to earn the title Alexander the Bicornous.

Stirred by Alexander's victorious deeds and his bloodlust, the demons expelled from heavens and biding in exile on earth believed him to be the Promised Beast who would open earth's portals to destruction and restore the vaults of heavens to their tribe. They gathered around him and with their whisperings urged him to conquer the heavens, and to lay claim to it as his dominion, so that they could again have unimpeded access there. They contrived for him a throne to be flown by four chained griffins lured upwards with bait. Their persuasions and machinations made Alexander full of ambition to conquer the heavens. He set out on his journey with the griffins flying his throne, and climbed to such a height that the earth appeared to him a blue glass orb, and the sea like a writhing serpent.

Seeing Alexander trespass upon their domain, the guardians of the first heaven defended it, hurling fiery stones and lightning bolts at him. Alexander fell to the ground in ignominy, weighed down by grief at his failure. He did not know that his life had been spared for he was destined to do a certain deed on earth.

Undeterred by their defeat in the plan to conquer the heavens, the demons pointed the end of land to Alexander, and filled his head with plans to conquer and add to his dominions the mighty sea which none had vanquished before. They brought a diving machine for Alexander, built by their sea brethren and propelled by the power of stars, to travel underwater and take the measure of the sea. Ambition and vanity again stirred in

Alexander's head, and he set out to survey and subdue the sea's empire. He travelled underwater in the demons' machine for a long while without surfacing. He saw many a sight, and encountered many a monster. One of the latter was the tanneen that causes the waves to form in the sea with its motion. It is said that the tanneen saw in Alexander his own evil reflection and attacked him, shattering the demonic machine and injuring Alexander gravely. But Alexander's life was spared yet again for he was destined to do a certain deed on earth.

The darkness and terrors of the deep sea had struck fear in Alexander's heart. He gave up the ambition to conquer it and never plumbed its depths again nor sailed over it.

It is related that in his last days Alexander surveyed the world and his conquests, and learned that there was one corner of earth where his sword and writ had not yet reached. In order to complete his conquest, he marched at the head of a mighty phalanx to where the East began.

When he arrived there he found two high mountains whose foothills were inhabited by many an ascetic and philosopher. The mountains were a shield between them and a race of sanguinary creatures who issued forth from a narrow pass between the mountains to ravage their lands, kill their people, and take away their kine. The sages entreated Alexander to protect them from these creatures, and offered him their allegiance in perpetuity in return for his help.

Alexander went towards the pass between those mighty mountains and after crossing it regarded the race of Gog and Magog, named after two brothers—the progeny of Japheth, son of Noah—who made their home in those mountains after the floodwaters receded. Their faces and upper bodies were like humans but they varied greatly in stature. Some were tall, some measured a yard high, and yet others a handspan. They had fangs, talons instead of nails, and short, hairy tails. Like animals, they went about naked, fornicated openly, and voided their bowels copiously like beasts.

The Gog and Magog possessed neither faith nor a tradition, were unacquainted with any gods, and seldom heard the tread of death amidst them, as none of them died before witnessing a thousand generations born of his progeny.

Alexander gathered a host of men and the tribe of demons and ordered them to set about making a Rampart against Gog and Magog. At first, the demons refused to construct the Rampart because it hindered their life's purpose to create strife, but Alexander used his sword and powerful spells to make them submit to him.

The demons brought sheets of iron and piled them one upon the other, until they had risen high as the two mountains, encircling them like a Rampart. They lit fires underneath the iron sheets, and when they became red hot, poured molten copper over them, which settled in the grooves and became solid and unimpregnable, so that none could climb the Rampart nor make a hole through it. The Rampart was thirty-six leagues in length and five cubits in thickness. It would hold against Gog and Magog until the End Time.

Disappointed in Alexander the demons left him to search for another who could be a tool for fulfilling their impious ambitions.

From the time Alexander has imprisoned them, Gog and Magog daily try to break through the Rampart. Having no implements or weapons with which to breach it, they lick it with their abrasive tongues, and keep at it from sunrise to sunset until the Rampart becomes thin as eggshell. Their armies then retire to rest, vowing to resume work upon the following morn. But the Creator so wills that the Rampart regains its thickness overnight, and the following day Gog and Magog have to resume their labours all over again. Towards the End Time, however, a child will be born among them who will rise to become their commander. One day he will break loose from the Rampart, and travel into the world to gather all the demons who had once followed Alexander, to form an army and finally stamp out humanity from the world.

With the completion of the Rampart Alexander had accomplished the good deed he was destined to do on earth. He cast off the mortal coil as his account in the ledger of existence was closed.

∽

While Alexander lived and was planning his conquest of the sea, a mermaid swam into the waters close to the shores of Greece. Although a child of Cain, the ancestor of all brutes and fiends, she was neither marked with lumps on her forehead, cheeks and hands, nor at all unsightly. Of beautiful eyes, flowing hair, and ruddy breasts, she had the full form of a woman on land, and in water the lower body of a fish, so she could travel both on land and in water with grace.

She was swimming one day, when a glass carriage, propelled by the power of stars, came through the sea. It passed by her and she saw inside it a princely youth whose majestic demeanour made her besotted with love for him. He made his observations of the sea depth and its beasts but saw not the mermaid, and returned whence he had come. She followed him to the shore and learned from the singers of legends and the composers of ballads that the mysterious youth in the glass carriage was none other than Alexander, a great monarch who had conquered both East and West with his horse, measured the heavens' expanse in his chariot of griffins, and now fathomed the sea in his glass carriage to plan its conquest. Hearing of his glorious deeds made the mermaid love him the more fervently.

At the same time and in the same sea that the mermaid swam, and sighted the glass carriage in which Alexander rode, there also swam a young sorcerer studying the four elements: water, earth, air, and fire. He had by then mastered only water.

The sorcerer had seen the mermaid as she stopped to watch the glass carriage, and became transfixed with wonder by her beauty. They stood opposite each other under the sea as Alexander's glass carriage went past them. The sorcerer wished the mermaid to look at him so that he could read his fortune in her eyes. But although they stood facing each other for some time, she neither saw nor became aware of the sorcerer, who watched her disconsolately as her eyes followed Alexander.

Returning to the sea restless and melancholy, the mermaid sought me, Apollonius of Tyana, and beseeched me for a talisman—in the name of my power over the seven planets which hovered above the lives of creatures and coloured them with sorrow and joy—to join her fate with Alexander's life.

The young sorcerer learned that the trappings of power held sway over the mermaid's heart. Frenzied in his desire to obtain it, he, too, beseeched me for a talisman that would open to him the archives of cosmic learning and the crypts and sealed vaults where dark knowledge was concealed so that he could use it to accumulate power to find his way into her heart.

I looked into the folios of their fate and felt pity for both the mermaid and sorcerer. I know the loving heart and also recognize vanity and its false quests. With spells that invoke causes and effects, I wrought a talisman in which the Past, Present and Future merged. I ordained new fates, and with separation and ordeals bound both the mermaid and sorcerer together in this talisman which would yoke them to an eternal search for power and glory.

I witnessed the mermaid finally discovering the falsity of what she sought. With her fate tied to Alexander, she lived the fate of all the women who fell in love with him, and whose love was not answered, for Alexander's lust for conquest had made his heart desolate. Rather than discover the infinitude of love's eternal glory, he preferred to extend with the sword his dominion, and erect with stone and mortar new edifices to his mortality. The mermaid could not break free from her fate to which this talisman had fettered her.

I regarded the young sorcerer, too. With time, he attained power over the elements and Time by conquering the seven planets with powerful invocations. Like all great sorcerers he, too, created new astrological statuettes so that he held a key to the planets' magic. He established his rule over water, a kingdom vaster, and more populous and magnificent than Alexander's, who had failed to conquer it.

The sorcerer had grown in conceit from his great learning, which bred in him a vanity he had not before felt. Arrogance and love cannot abide together, and while he still sometimes thought of the mermaid with a vague longing, he no longer remembered her with a lover's tender self-effacement, nor desired her with the same urgent passion. He lost his original purpose, and with it his desire. Like Alexander, his search for a vain fulfillment became a bane. From his lust for glory he deformed into a half-beast.

∽

Finally, Qazwini came upon the enigmatic last words of the text:

Like all constructs of magic the *Book of Power*, too, has a key. I, Apollonius of Tyana, aver that in time, the ordeal written in this talisman will bring the mermaid and sorcerer together. The vanity in their hearts that had separated them shall come unbound, what had fallen into darkness be brought into light, and the two destined to find love reunited, if the master of this *Book of Power* should spurn the cursed rewards of power and consign it to the dominion where the mermaid and the sorcerer had first met, and where their fates were rewritten into this talisman.

—*Book of Power*

Chapter 59

After reading the compact, Qazwini had wondered if by keeping the grimoire in his possession he would place himself under the compact as well. One night as he slept, Qazwini had his first apocalyptic dream. It revealed to him the vision of the creature behind Alexander's Rampart.

Qazwini beheld a creature come towards him as a swarm of beings, moving like a molten mass in the darkness, hissing, chirping, and rattling as he advanced. Reeking of violence, the composite being of nightmares and fears emerged into his view. The smaller beings were a part of it and carried him forward. Wailing and howling cloaked him and visions of destruction followed in his wake. A procession of spirits smelling of rotting flesh led the way with burning torches. Sandstorms and dark gales swept the land where he set foot. This was the glorious progeny of violent ambition and intelligence that must always reorder the world with destruction; the parricide who destroyed equally the man who sired him, and the time which gave him birth. A pair of glowing eyes lit the dark void of the being's face and regarded Qazwini from the bounded darkness, before the outlines spread, becoming fiery letters that read: *The Promise that is made shall be kept and this gate levelled by the hands whose work is not immediately manifest.* The creature advanced towards Qazwini until the suffocating terror ended his sleep.

The answer had finally become clear to Qazwini as to why the Abbasids remained preoccupied with End Time events since coming into the *Book of Power* and why they would not give up its possession. The caliphs understood that the only way their power could be destroyed would be through the End Time creatures Gog and Magog. They carefully investigated every report of the End Time creatures and held on to the *Book of Power* which, they believed, would protect them. In the end it was the evil associated with acquisition of power itself that worked the destruction of the Abbasids. Their trust in a power other than God weakened them in the face of the Adversary determined to dominate the human world.

Qazwini had spent much time reflecting on the battle of Ain Jalut in which many of Juvayni's men had been killed and recalling Duraid's prophecy about the Mongols' destruction. It was the first instance after their conquest of Baghdad that the invincible Mongols had been checked and repulsed in their progress. The *Book of Power* had been under Mongol possession for a time, even though the fact was not known to them.

Chapter 60

Qazwini stood by the Tigris in whose waters he had drowned the *Book of Power*. The last person to have held the key to power had recognized that it must be destroyed to put to sleep forever the evil it stirred.

For power to be wielded judiciously, it had to be employed with the knowledge of the cause it served and the adversary it sought to eliminate. The spells and talismans contained within the book gave one power over elements and men, and Qazwini felt he could wield it with profit in his life. But power was a trust a human wielded as God's vicegerent, and when it was illegitimate it only attracted other malfeasant aspirants and their mischief. Qazwini was sure that the nature of glory bestowed by the *Book of Power* was unsanctioned, and any accomplishments obtained with its help would remain unredeemed.

∽

Consigned to water, the spell had come unbound. As Qazwini stood there, unbeknown to him, the ink from the folios of the *Book of Power* submerged in water gathered, and moved away from the shore like a dark-bodied creature escaping. Its darkening body summoned to its expanse the mighty power of winds, the rage of sea waves, and the maddening terrors of the sea, to become a tempest. It spread and built momentum as it moved from the Tigris into the Persian Gulf seeking something.

Chapter 61

The gale had come upon them with scant warning. The growl of thunder and the fierce music of wind blasting through the galley's apertures seemed the finale of the sinister melody that held in a dreadful vice the hearts of the soldiers and seamen. The cause of turbulence lay in the noisy darkness, which had engulfed them. It began with the water turning murky until it was fully impenetrable to the gaze.

The seamen at first thought that the darkening waters around the galley were the portent of a great leviathan surfacing. To drive it away they had blown on their horns and mightily beat the kettledrums, but the water's surface remained unbroken by bubbles. The sails were brailed up for fear of a tempest rising from the depths and engulfing them. The blackness surrounding them moved apace with the galley—a dark steed rushing them to some sinister destiny.

The mercenaries and seamen aboard had made ambuscades and escapes with the guidance of the stars and favourable winds, and were familiar with the horrors of the terraqueous world, but this unknown phenomenon had filled them with terrible foreboding. They whispered that it was a continuation of the evil that had been afoot since the mysterious wooden box had been loaded aboard the galley. The labourers who carried it aboard were frightened by the growls they heard from it, and left the galley in panic. At night, the sailors heard a droning sound from the hold where it lay. Nobody dared touch it lest he should invite the wrath of the Baghdad governor whose seal marked it as official property.

With the stars hidden, the gale in its ripest temper, and the galley's navigation given to the call of fate, the darkness began to communicate with them. The soft creaking noises from the galley's wooden sides and decks, mistaken in the beginning for the imminent dismembering of the vessel by some beast of the depths, began to sound like plaintive cries. Those who listened with ears to the planks could also hear distant, muffled growls, the terrifying address of some creature that echoed in their bones.

One day, soon after sunset, the ship come to a standstill. On the deck, loud noises were heard that abruptly died, and a powerful symphony of barks and baying broke upon the ship. Filled with the presentiment that the feared and fated had come to pass, the men in the hold climbed to the deck with the help of rope ladders, and froze at the sight that met them.

The darkness around the ship had shrunk and coalesced at the ship's prow in the form of a creature bathed in luminosity with the face and upper body of a woman and the lower body of a fish. Towering above the ship's prow, she was far more ravishing than any mermaid ever seen. Her hands secured the prow around which her elongated lower body coiled like a snake. A pack of aquatic dogs circled below noisily. Their clamour had reached the sailors in the hold earlier, muffled by the wooden planks.

Above, the dark clouds had shrunk, like the dark water around the ship, and her scales reflected the amber glare hanging over the sky. Her eyes were fixed on the horizon's shiny glass.

'Did vanity and love abide together, ever?' the mermaid called out, in a wistful voice. The voice hurt those who heard it like an echo of pain. Those gathered near the prow felt the fierce glow of her aspect upon them, although she neither spoke nor looked at anyone. The seamen exchanged bewildered glances and confused mutterings. Deep in the galley's hold the terror-stricken slaves heard a banging grow louder from within the wooden box, as if someone had the answer for the mermaid. None dared approach it to investigate.

The woman of the sea again uttered a cry, and the ship lurched violently as her hands steered the prow, sending those standing on deck hurtling and crashing against wood, metal, and ropes. The barking of the aquatic dogs became deafening.

A loud growl accompanied by the splash of something heavy falling from the deck into the sea introduced a booming silence. In the hold the wooden box had fallen silent.

The woman of the sea flapped her fish tail in the water and the ship's movement became calm. Before the men on deck could even move from where they stood, she had sunk into the sea amid the darkness that heralded her, as if she had been an illusion.

Those manning the galley's bank of oars saw a man with the body of a fish emerge from the water and give out a loud bark. At his call, a woman and a child who were from his race emerged from the water and quickly swam towards him.

They briefly came together before diving into the dark water and disappearing from view.

The galley rowed on.

When the cargo was unloaded from the galley at Constantinople, the wooden box was found to be empty. Whatever was inside had escaped. The galley's captain was grateful that he was saved any penalties for the lost cargo, as nobody came to claim the box until they raised anchor.

Epilogue

Juvayni's work on his universal history never progressed beyond the year Gujastak was produced in his court. The ongoing campaign against the Mamluks, attending to the dispatches from commanders, and helping set up supply routes, along with his daily duties as governor occupied his nights and days. The impediments to his own work daily grew and kept him from returning to his work on his book. Whenever he returned to it, both words and memory failed him. He ended the book where it lay, unfinished. As an example of frustrated ambition, Juvayni's resplendent universal history, *History of the World Conqueror*, remained one of the world's greatest unfinished histories. To the end of his days he felt it was either a curse or the revenge of the theologians' disturbed souls, whose vestiges in the Wisdom Chamber he had destroyed.

Little benefit had come to Qazwini from his experiment. His treatise, *The Mysterious Life of Merman Gujastak*, in which he had written a detailed nomenclature of Gujastak, was lost to time. He had prepared it as a prelude to a more detailed work, never attempted. He had already shelved an earlier allegorical work, *The Perfidy of the Left Rib*, on the unruly passions of women, and never returned to that either.

The marvellous transformations of Aydan and Gujastak witnessed by him remained an unexplained marvel to Qazwini. Qazwini had dismissed as too far-fetched the thought that Gujastak and Aydan were a talismanic manifestation of the sorcerer and mermaid from the *Book of Power*.

Until his end, Qazwini could not ascertain what purpose the beast-humans served in the human universe. He did not consider it a defeat of reason in the service of faith, merely a demonstration that some enquiries into the marvels of God may remain unanswered; if reason could encompass all of God's mysteries, it would obliterate the capacity for wonder that was fundamental to how the Creator expressed His power over his creatures.

Until Qazwini's writing of his celebrated cosmography, *Marvels of Things Created and Miraculous Aspects of Things Existing*, which earned him the reputation of the greatest natural historian and cosmographer of his day, he was remembered in Baghdad streets in the role of Gujastak's sterile wife in ribald verses.